# A Warrior Wedding

BY

*Teresa Gabelman*

A WARRIOR WEDDING

Gabelman, Teresa (18-8-2015). A WARRIOR WEDDING.

Published by: Indie Digital Publishing LLC

www.IndieDigitalPublishing.com

Paperback Edition.

Editor: Hot Tree Editing

Photo: iStockphoto

Cover Art: Indie Digital Publishing LLC - Ron Gabelman

www.teresagabelman.com

www.facebook.com/pages/Teresa-Gabelman/191553587598342

# Acknowledgement

Thank you to my editor Becky Johnson (Hot Tree Editing), Donna Pemberton, Donna Bossert, Emma Treadway, and Kelly Perkins. Without you this book wouldn't have happened. I am forever grateful and appreciate you more than you will ever know.

To all the readers…without you…there is no story!

# CHAPTER 1

Jill rushed through the drug store looking at the signs hanging from each aisle. She needed to hurry. Sloan wanted them back at his office fifteen minutes ago and, as usual, Steve was on the verge of a freak out. They had just finished target practice and she practically had to beg Adam to stop. No one wanted to walk into Sloan's office late. Well, maybe Sid, but that was Sid.

Seeing the aisle that she needed, she headed that way, her heart beating out of her chest as her stomach heaved painfully. Finding what she was looking for, she cursed. "Holy shit." Seriously, how many of these things were there?

An older woman strolled down the same aisle looking first at Jill, then to the products Jill was looking at, and then back to Jill, an understanding expression crossing her wrinkled face before moving on. Jill shifted uncomfortably. Once the woman had disappeared, Jill grabbed a box only to stare at it. She knew deep down this was impossible. It couldn't be, but she had to be sure.

"Five minutes?" Jill whispered as she read the box. She could have the answer in five minutes and then she would know for sure, what she already knew, but then again, since becoming a half-breed, things were not always what they seemed. Surprises were around every single corner she turned, and for a girl who used to like surprises, she now hated them with a passion.

"What in the hell are you doing?"

So deep in thought, Jill jumped, the box flying out of her hand as she turned. To her horror the box landed in Adam's hand. Reaching for it, she missed when he pulled it further away from her grabbing hands. Adam's eyes narrowed as Steve snatched the box.

"What is it?" Steve looked at the box for a few seconds before shock flashed across his face and he threw the box back to Adam. "What in the hell have you done, Jill?"

"It's not mine." Jill looked away quickly then back, indicating she was lying her ass off. When she saw the identical looks of 'calling her bullshit' on their faces, she sighed. "Just give it to me."

"What's going on?" Adam crossed his arms, while still holding the box.

"Yeah, inquiring minds want to know," Steve added, also crossing his arms and blocking her escape path. "What *is* going on?"

"There is no way you can be pregnant." Adam glared down at her. "So why were you buying this?"

"Yeah, there's no way...unless..." Steve's mouth formed an 'oh, shit' circle. "Slade's dead, but you're not. You're only half dead which means..."

"Which means what?" Jill growled, her eyes narrowing dangerously. When Steve just cocked an eyebrow at her, she grabbed another box from the shelf throwing it at him. "I'm not cheating on Slade, you ass."

"Then why do you need that?" Steve pointed at the box Adam held, then to the box on the floor before waving his hand at all the boxes on the shelves.

She knew she could blow Steve off, but Adam was a different matter. His penetrating gaze told her that he was not letting this go, and would stand there all day until she talked. Another woman started down the aisle, but spotted them and backtracked until she disappeared.

"I've been sick." Jill sighed and felt a little better saying it. "It started after the initiation and hasn't gotten any better."

"So you think you're pregnant?" Adam frowned. "We're half human, Jill. We can still get sick."

"Yeah." Steve looked a little less stressed. "You probably just have a virus or something. You do look like crap though. Maybe we can stop by the makeup aisle and get you something for those bags under your eyes."

Adam slowly turned his head toward Steve, his frown hard.

"What? I'm making an observation. She looks like crap." Steve looked back at Jill. "And now that we're on the subject, you've lost some weight. It could be water weight though."

"What in the *fuck* are you talking about?" Adam growled. He then closed his eyes with a shake of his head. "You know what, don't answer that."

Steve ignored him and answered anyway, "Women have water weight. So sometimes when they look like they've lost weight, it's just water weight. Not weight-weight." Turning his attention to Jill, he continued like he knew exactly what he was talking about, "Other than losing weight and those dark bags under your eyes, what else is going on with you?"

Jill actually touched under her eyes self-consciously, then cursed because she was actually listening to Steve. "I can't keep blood down," Jill replied, feeling weak just saying it. "I fed from Slade a couple days after initiation and it came right back up."

"What did he say?" Adam asked, but when she remained silent, he frowned. "You haven't told him?"

"No." Jill shuffled from one foot to the other. "He's been so busy with all the funeral ceremonies, I just thought like you guys do. I have a virus, but I'm not getting any better. Regular food makes me nauseous, but even if I eat a rare steak for the blood, it comes right back up."

"Ah, hello!" Steve threw his arms out wide. "You're engaged to a doctor."

Jill stared at Steve for a second before tugging the box out of Adam's hand and heading to the register.

"You need to tell Slade." Adam followed her. She could almost feel his frowning glare smacking her in the back of the head. "This doesn't sound normal."

"He's been so busy and"—Jill tossed the box on the counter to pay—"I don't want to bother him."

The woman behind the counter took the box, but was staring at Steve and Adam with disapproval as Jill dug money out of her pocket.

"Honey, you shouldn't be the one paying for this." The woman glared at Adam and Steve, who stood behind Jill with their arms crossed.

Steve's eyes widened as he stepped back from Jill, a mortified look on his face. "Whoa!" He looked around nervously as if Slade would pop out of the hair product aisle behind them. "I have absolutely nothing to do with…that!" He pointed to the box.

When the woman's eyes went to Adam, Adam just shook his head, but didn't say a word. Jill paid for her purchase, asking the woman to double bag the one item.

The ride was silent except for the radio playing. Jill's hands shook, making the plastic bag rattle. Dropping it in her lap, she stared out the window. Her fear choked her as if someone had their hands around her throat. Something was definitely wrong because she was never sick. Even as a human she was never sick. How she had hidden it from Slade was a miracle, because Slade missed nothing.

Jill knew she wasn't pregnant, yet in the back of her mind, she remembered when her mom was pregnant with Seth, throwing up constantly and all she did was sleep. Resting her head back on the headrest, her eyes closed. She was tired and weak. All she wanted to do was go to bed and never get up.

\*\*\*\*\*\*

She could hear her name being called, but she had to fight to pry her eyes open.

"Go get Slade!" Steve's worried voice broke through the darkness she was fighting out of.

"No!" Her voice croaked as her eyes finally opened to slits. "I'm fine. Just waking up. Give me a second. Geez, can no one take a nap around here?"

"We've been trying to wake you for ten minutes." Steve's voice was high-pitched with worry.

Jill straightened to sit up, willing her eyes to open all the way. "Steve, stop being dramatic."

"He's not being dramatic, Jill." Adam broke in, his eyes missing nothing. "We've been trying to wake you for *ten* minutes."

"So I'm tired," Jill grumbled. "Haven't you ever been tired?"

"Not since I've been turned," Adam added, backing away to let her out of the car. When she swayed, he steadied her. "You need to talk to Slade."

"I will." Jill nodded, stretching. "I just think all the stress from everything going on got to me. I never did handle stress well."

She knew by the look Steve and Adam gave her they weren't buying it and neither would Slade.

# CHAPTER 2

As soon as they made it inside the compound, her phone buzzed indicating a text. Quickly looking at it, she saw it was from Slade, wanting to know where she was. Putting her phone in the back pocket of her jeans, she tried to fit the bag with the pregnancy test in there too. But it wasn't going to work. Wrapping the plastic bag around the test, she made sure no one could see what was inside. There was no way she could put off going to Sloan's office any longer. Hearing Adam and Steve's phone go off and their quickening steps, she knew they were really late and an ass chewing was only minutes away. Just what she didn't need.

Following them into the office, she glanced around. Slade stood leaning against the wall, his intense stare following her. She gave him a smile, but didn't head his way. Instead she followed Adam, her gaze finding Sloan who sat behind his desk, surprisingly not glaring or chewing their asses out.

The tenseness of the Warriors surrounded her, but Sloan seemed at ease sitting behind his desk staring at her. Okay, something was definitely off.

"It's about damn time," Sid grumbled, glaring at all three of them. "Where in the fuck have you been?"

"Jill had to get…" Steve started, but Jill stopped him by stepping on the back of his shoe. "Dammit, Jill."

"Sorry." Jill's eyes narrowed in warning at Steve who bent to put his shoe back on, his eyes meeting hers. The warning in her stare was clear. He needed to shut the hell up or else. Her eyes once again found Slade who hadn't moved an inch, but his gaze had become more intense. He knew. What he knew, she didn't know, but he knew something. Dammit.

"Sorry we're late." Steve walked toward Sloan's desk, without looking Sloan in the eye.

"No problem," Sloan replied and eyed Steve, Adam and Jill closely.

Everyone in the room stopped what they were doing to stare at Sloan.

"Who the fuck are you and what have you done with Sloan Murphy?" Sid glared at Sloan as if searching his soul.

Unease slithered down Jill's spine when she searched Sloan's eyes. This easy-going guy sitting behind Sloan's desk looked like Sloan, sounded like Sloan, but that was where it ended. He sure as hell wasn't acting like Sloan.

"What?" Sloan leaned back in his chair, crossing his arms.

Jill actually felt every Warrior in the room tense. Slade slowly moved toward her. Again her eyes moved to Sloan, but the office door slammed open, drawing everyone's attention. What she saw was something she hoped everyone else saw. If not, she really was sick...at least in the head.

"What the hell is going on?" Sloan's voice boomed as he stopped right inside his office.

Guns were drawn, half aimed at the Sloan behind the desk and the other at the Sloan glaring at them from his doorway.

"Eenie meenie miney mo, which Sloan has got to fucking go?" Sid's voice rang out, his gun pointed at the Sloan behind the desk, but looking over his shoulder at the Sloan in the doorway.

"You better have a damn good reason to have those guns pointed at me." Sloan took a step, as if daring any one of them to pull the trigger, but stopped when he saw his twin sitting behind his desk looking directly at him. "You have got to be fucking kidding me," was all he said as he continued to stare at the other Sloan.

"Everyone needs to calm down," the Sloan behind the desk said, starting to stand, but stopped as the sound of triggers clicking echoed in the room.

Jill watched the situation wishing she had her gun; she'd catch hell for that, but her mind had been preoccupied lately. She finally noticed Jax, who stood in the corner of the room, an arrogant half-grin on his face looking way too at ease with no gun drawn.

"Don't order my men around, motherfucker. If you Warriors don't stop aiming those fucking guns at me, you will be getting them surgically removed from your goddamn asses!" The Sloan by the doorway growled loud enough that Jill swore the room shook.

The Warriors, without moving an inch, looked at each other for a split second before all guns were turned and aimed toward the Sloan behind the desk. That was when all hell broke loose. Jill was pushed back when the Warriors, as one, took the Sloan doppelganger to the ground.

"You going to fucking do something?" The impersonator shouted.

Jill watched Jax slowly move away, his eyes meeting hers briefly. "Let him go." Jax's voice was smooth and calm.

Jared and Sid jerked the man up to a standing position, holding him tight, and Jill gasped. The man no longer looked like Sloan. His black hair hung in his eyes shielding them from view, but his massive frame loomed over Jared and Sid. He shook his head, finally revealing golden eyes framed by long black lashes. His fine muscled arms were sleeved with the most beautiful tattoos Jill had ever seen. She loved tats, but was too chicken to get one herself because pain sucked. Yeah, shock made her think of dumb shit.

When Jared and Sid didn't let go, the man growled loudly and shook them off. Sid re-pulled his gun aiming at the man's head.

"If someone doesn't start explaining, I'm going to unload in two seconds." Sid's voice was not the easy-going tone he usually expressed.

The man turned to Sid, bending slightly so the barrel pressed against his forehead. "Pull the trigger. I dare you."

"Good thing you didn't double dog dare him." Jared sneered. Everyone in the room became even more tense, if that were possible. "I'd hate to have my favorite shirt splattered with your brain matter, dumbass."

Sid's eyes darkened as he pushed the gun harder, making the man's head move slightly as he leaned closer. "Any last words?"

"Yeah." The man also leaned into the gun. "You're a pussy. Pull the trigger."

Sloan reacted by knocking the gun away before landing a punch to the man's face, then picked him up by the throat shoving him against the wall. "You have exactly one second to tell me who the fuck you are and why you shifted to look like me, which I never want to happen again or I will take your life with no questions asked."

The man cocked his eyebrow before hissing as Sloan's hand tightened painfully around his throat.

"I brought him in," Jax spoke up, still looking at ease and not at all put out by the situation that had everyone else on edge. "Blaze is not only an ex-Warrior, but a highly intelligent shifter."

"I wouldn't say he's too intelligent in the position he's in now." Steve snorted then stepped way back when Blaze's eyes narrowed on him.

"You going to let go of my throat?" His raspy voice from short air supply echoed in the room. Everyone waited to see what Sloan would do.

A rare sinister smile formed on Sloan's lips. "Not until you agree to never impersonate me or any of my men." Sloan's grin left his face quickly as his lip tilted into a snarl. Blaze struggled, but Sloan, even though just a bit smaller than the man, didn't lose his grip. "And even then I'll think about it."

"It was his brilliant idea," Blaze hissed out, his eyes betraying Jax.

Finally, after what seemed like hours, Sloan pushed away from the man, letting his death grip go before turning on Jax. "Explain," he demanded, walking around his desk, everyone giving him plenty of space. Jill tripped over her own feet backing out of Sloan's way. She had never seen him so pissed.

Jax didn't seem the least bit upset that Blaze ratted him out. "I wanted to prove to everyone how easy it is for someone to shift and impersonate any one of you. Until now, I don't think you guys totally understood. Now you do."

"He didn't shimmer," Jill pointed out. "Don't they usually shimmer before they shift?"

Blaze snorted, but his eyes pinned her to the spot. "I don't shimmer." His words were hard and deep.

"And that's exactly why I brought him in," Jax replied. "My brother is up to something and honestly, we need more help finding him. Blaze is the best and is an ex-Warrior. He knows a lot of people in both the vampire and shifter circles. We need him and he agreed to help."

"Ex-Warrior?" Steve glanced at the large man whose head swiveled toward him. "You get kicked out or something?"

At first it didn't look like Blaze was going to answer, but a humorless grin curved his lips. "Or something." His eyes went to Adam and then Jill. "So when did the VC Warriors start letting boys and women join the ranks?"

Adam didn't say a word, but the tick in his jaw indicated he heard loud and clear. Jill on the other hand took offense, as usual. "With a name like Blaze, I'm surprised you don't shimmer." She rolled her eyes. "Seriously, who names their kid Blaze? You got a brother named Inferno?"

Sid and Jared smiled proudly, looking as if they were going to pat Jill on the head knowing they had taught her well in the art of being a smartass. Blaze, on the other hand, didn't smile at all, but his eyes took on a funny swirly motion as he glared at Jill.

"Little girl, you best be careful and learn some manners before speaking of things you know nothing about." Blaze's lip tilted in a sinister grin as his eyes continued to swirl.

Jill became lost in his crazy gaze and couldn't pull her eyes away. A burning heat started in the pit of her stomach inching along her spine, through her body slowly, until it reached her neck. She swayed and heard her name, but couldn't open her mouth to respond. The edges of her sight started to darken as if looking through a pin hole into this man's wicked gaze. In a final whoosh, her vision went black, while the heat in her body intensified, and that was all she knew.

# CHAPTER 3

"Jill!" Slade's voice sounded far away. Jill did everything she could to claw her way to him, but the darkness kept a tight hold over her. "Jill, wake up, dammit." Why did Slade sound so pissed. Was he mad at her?

Fighting hard to break out of the darkness that gripped her, Jill pried her eyes open to slits, but moaned at the brightness. "I'm up," she croaked, licking her dry lips. "Stop yelling at me. I'm up."

She felt Slade's large hand as it rested against her forehead while he pried one eyelid open.

"What are you doing?" She weakly pushed his hand away.

"Hold still." Slade's voice was stern with a hint of worry, and that was when it all came back to her in a flash.

This time, she succeeded in pushing his hand away as she sat up a little too quickly. Everything inside her revolted at the movement and she dry-heaved herself right off the table. If not for Slade, she would have landed face first on the floor.

"Find out what that son of a bitch did to her," Slade ordered someone in the room. She heard the door slam and realized she was in Slade's office.

Getting her stomach under control, Jill opened her eyes, letting Slade help her up and back onto the table. "I'm okay."

"No, she's not," Steve answered from behind her.

"Shut up, Steve." Jill turned toward him, giving him a warning glare. "I said I'm fine."

Before Steve could reply, the door opened and in came Blaze along with Sloan, Jax, and Sid. In a split second, claustrophobia set in with the huge Warriors in Slade's small office all staring at her.

"What did you do to her?" Slade kept one hand on Jill's leg to keep her steady as he pushed his face toward Blaze's.

Blaze didn't lean back, but his eyes did shoot to Jill's before looking back at Slade. "What I did should not have had that effect on her."

"I asked you a question, not your opinion." Slade's voice turned deadly.

"Slade, I'm fine." Jill grabbed onto his hand that tightened on her leg.

"And I repeat, no, she's not," Steve added, ignoring Jill's death glare.

Slade glanced at her for a split second, his eyes searching hers. "Why do you say that, Steve?"

Jill sighed, rolling her eyes, ready to open her mouth, but Steve beat her to it.

"She's been getting sick. She can't hold down blood and—"

"I probably have a virus or something." Jill felt every eye on her as she interrupted blabbermouth. She hated attention directed toward her. It made her more nauseous than she already was, and then she heard a plastic bag rattle. Her heart sunk as her stomach rose to the back of her throat.

Steve reached into the plastic bag. "So tell me, Doc, do women with viruses usually get pregnancy tests? It took us ten minutes to wake her up once we got here today, and she looks like shit." He looked at Jill, raising an eyebrow. "Well, you do."

"You're an asshole," Jill sneered at Steve.

"Yeah, well, I'm more afraid of him"—he nodded at Slade—"than I am of you. He needed to know and I have diarrhea of the mouth when I'm afraid of something, as you well know. And that big bastard scares the hell out of me. Oh, and just to make sure everyone in this room knows, if she is pregnant, I had absolutely nothing to do with it."

Slade took the pregnancy test from Steve, looking at it then to Jill without saying a word. The room went deathly quiet.

"Annnnd, on that note,"—Sid edged toward the door—"we're out. You need us for anything, Slade, just…." The door shut muffling anything else Sid had to say as everyone emptied out of the room as if it were on fire. Even Sloan exited the room without a word spoken.

Jill's eyes rose to look at Slade, who was staring at the pregnancy test in his large hand. "Listen, I know I'm not—"

"Why didn't you tell me you were sick?" Slade's tone was flat, neither angry nor…actually, it was just flat, no emotion whatsoever, and she didn't like it.

"I really didn't think it was anything and it probably isn't," Jill began, but could tell he didn't believe her. She started to fidget on the table when he remained silent. "And…I didn't want to bother you." She finally admitted the real reason she hadn't told him.

"I'm not like your family, Jill." Finally Slade's voice held some emotion, angry emotion, but it was emotion.

"I know that," she replied, no longer sure she believed her words. Why hadn't she told him right away she was sick? Had she been afraid he would toss her aside because she was being a pain in the ass? She knew that was exactly the problem, and by the look on Slade's face, he knew it too.

"Do you truly believe you're pregnant?" Slade pointed the test at her. "Because if you are pregnant, there is a dead man walking out there who I need to find."

Warmth flushed her body at his words and she shook her head. "I haven't been with anyone but you," she whispered.

"Then you're not pregnant." Slade tossed the test in the garbage can. "I want to know everything, and I mean *everything*, from the beginning till tonight. If you leave anything out, I will bust your ass. You hear me?" He growled the question at her.

"Yes, I hear you." Jill nodded. Usually, she would be a little more of a smartass when answering to his attitude, but she just wasn't up to it. She was ready to find out what in the hell was wrong with her and since Steve, the narc, told on her, she was ready to let it all out.

"Are you okay?" Slade walked up to stand in front of her, his large hand feeling her forehead, then running down her neck while feeling the pulse in her throat.

She nodded, leaning into his hand. "I'm fi…" She started to say, but his narrowed eyes told her he knew she was about to lie. "I'm feeling a little weak."

"Do you need to feed?" The concern in his voice was palpable.

"I don't know." She shrugged one shoulder. "I just fed from you, but I couldn't keep it down and while real food stays down, it makes me so nauseous that I'd rather go without."

He tilted her face up to his. "You need to feed." It was a demand, not a suggestion.

"I can't keep taking your blood and then vomiting it up." Jill responded with a frown. "It's too good to waste."

A small grin tipped his lips, but didn't reach his eyes as he turned away from her, looking through a few drawers in the metal cabinets behind him. "I need to take some blood."

Jill wrapped her arms around her waist with a sour grimace. "How much do you have to take?"

"Three vials." He turned toward her, his hands filled with everything he needed. He set everything down behind her. Putting his hands on each side of her legs, Slade caged her on the table and leaned in close. "You never look like that when my teeth are sinking into your sweet, soft neck. This is the same thing."

Jill stared up at him. "It's so not the same thing, Slade." She actually blushed. He was the only person who could make her blush.

His sexy lips tilted in a smile as he winked at her. His mouth took hers hard. His hands remained on the table, but hers clutched him as if he were her lifeline.

All too soon his lips left hers leaving her breathless.

"You ready?" His dark eyes stared down at her.

"No," she replied, but nodded.

"I love you." His deep voice washed over her and still he didn't move, but stared steadily at her with his intense gaze. "I will not let anything happen to you."

Swallowing hard, she nodded again. "I'm sorry I didn't tell you sooner." She did feel guilty about not coming to him when it first started, especially since he was being so sweet.

A frown flashed across his face. "We will deal with that issue as soon as we find out what's going on and you feel better," he warned her.

Relief crossed her face, but his frown didn't disappear.

"I won't forget, Jill." His tone definitely indicated he wouldn't forget and it would be dealt with, but usually his punishments were awesomely blissful in the end. She shivered in a good way at the thought.

She kept quiet as he grabbed what he needed to take blood. With hands so large, he was surprisingly gentle as he wrapped the tourniquet around her arm. She watched until he reached for the thing with the needle. Lifting her head, she stared straight ahead. She hated the thing with the needle.

"Make a fist," he ordered, his voice deep and strong.

16

She watched his handsome face instead of what he was doing to her arm. Her free hand clawed the table in a death grip waiting for the painful pinch of the needle. She knew her body was tense, but she couldn't help it. It was either that or cry like a little bitch, and she didn't want to do that in front of him. She heard plastic ripping and crinkling knowing it was coming. His eyes finally met hers.

"You need to relax." His intense gaze searched hers then fell to her lips. "I only have to stick you once and I'm very good at what I do. Just a small pinch and it's over."

Taking a deep breath, she nodded. She knew what it felt like to get blood taken and knew he was lying his ass off. It hurt like hell. "Go for it." She squeezed her eyes closed, biting her lip.

"Stop biting your lip, Jill," he demanded. "I have plans for those later."

Her eyes popped open in surprise and he made his move. The needle slid into her arm and yeah, it hurt like hell. "That was dirty." Jill hissed as her eyes automatically went to what hurt her, then shot back to his grinning face.

"It worked." Arrogance laced his words.

"No, it didn't." She glared at him. "It hurt like hell, just like when you set my shoulder on the count of two, not three. I didn't think doctors were supposed to lie to their patients."

"I wasn't lying. I do have plans for those lips later." His darkening eyes promised many things as he pulled the needle out, and placed something over the small puncture wound before bending her arm. "Hold your arm like that and don't move it." He took the three vials, placing them each in small envelopes.

Her body burned at his words. Even nauseous and feeling like dog crap, the thought of being with him was heaven. She had turned into such a Warrior whore. She snickered at the thought. Giving him a once over, she knew she couldn't wait until tonight. Sliding off the table, keeping her arm folded up, she walked up to him and touched his back.

"What kind of plans?" She loved the feel of his strong body and would never get enough of it.

"Well, that all depends on the blood test." He turned, taking her into his arms. "I'm going to head to the hospital now while you go to our room and rest. Then we'll see what happens."

Jill huffed. "You're a tease."

"No, I'm a doctor who loves you." He tilted her face up to meet his, placing a kiss to her frowning lips. "And my main job is to make sure you're okay."

Jill nodded, pulling away. "Fine, I'll go up to our room and take care of…things…and then rest." If he could tease, so could she.

In an instant, she was back in his arms. "I don't think so." He growled. "I take care of your needs, always. You keep your hands to yourself until I get back. You understand?"

Jill bobbed her head, but cocked her eyebrow. Like he would know.

"Oh, I'll know." He answered her thoughts, shocking her, which was something he was good at doing. "Never doubt that."

Giving him a kiss and a glare, she pushed away from him. "You're cruel."

"Get some rest," Slade ordered. "I want to find you in bed, resting and…"

"Unsatisfied." She finished for him as she slammed the door behind her. "Jerk," she whispered, but grinned, feeling better than she had in days. Maybe Steve and Adam were right. Just letting Slade know what was going on took some of the stress off her, making her feel better. It had to be stress making her sick, but deep down, she knew it wasn't that simple.

# CHAPTER 4

As soon as the door closed behind Jill, Slade's grin quickly formed into a frown. Worry marred his handsome features. Turning, he grabbed his phone and put in a quick call to the hospital. Someone knocked on the door before it opened. Slade held up his hand as he grabbed the envelopes with Jill's blood.

"I'll be there in fifteen. I appreciate it." He hung up turning. "What the fuck do you want?"

"Is she okay?" Blaze stood just inside the door, his golden eyes not looking away from Slade's deadly glare.

Realizing he still didn't know what the hell this asshole did to her, Slade set down her precious blood in a safe place. "What did you do to her?" His voice was even, but held an edge of 'answer up or face the consequences.'

Blaze's eyes darkened slightly at the unspoken threat. "She questioned my name and I showed her." When Slade continued to stare, he continued. "I have the unique power of setting things on fire."

Slade straightened, the veins in his neck throbbing, his face seething with fury. "And you thought it was a good idea to teach my mate a lesson about your fucking name by setting her on fire. Bad move, motherfucker." Slade sneered as his eyes turned black, his hands fisted and with no Jill lying unconscious on the floor distracting him and no one to separate them, he unleashed on Blaze.

The men pounded on each other, Slade was impressed by the other man's abilities, but his worry over Jill gave him the advantage.

"I didn't set her on fire." Blaze growled as he evaded a punch landing one of his own. "Only made her feel a little heat. I'm a bastard, but I would never hurt an innocent woman, just teach her some manners."

"You teach my mate nothing, and if you ever put her in harm's way again, I will kill you without a second thought." With one last punch to Blaze's gut and an upper cut to his chin, Slade finally sat the big bastard on his ass.

Blaze looked up at Slade as if he wanted to say something, but stopped himself. With a nod, he stood and wiped the blood from his mouth. Walking out the door, he added, "I'll honor your request, but stay the fuck out of my face."

Slade stared at the empty doorway. "Then don't piss me off." He didn't care if the fucker heard him or not. Slade touched his eye. Pulling his hand away, blood stained his fingers. He cursed. He had more important matters to take care of. Grabbing the envelopes off the desk, he picked up his keys and headed out the door, the feeling of dread following his every footstep. He hoped to hell he was mistaken, but clutching his mate's life in his hands, he had a bad feeling he was far from wrong.

******

Jill didn't really disobey Slade. She was resting in the kitchen trying to stomach some warm Pepsi and crackers. So far so good. Nothing was coming up and her stomach seemed calm. It was rare to be in the kitchen alone. Looking around, she still couldn't believe she was living in the VC Warrior compound and was an actual active Warrior. She was surrounded by good people who cared for her, had a man who never in her wildest dreams thought would have give her a second look, and that alone made her realize how lucky she was. She was a half-breed vampire against her will, but the end result was she had found her soul mate. Slade was everything to her and she felt she was everything to him. Even with their relationship being new, her love for him was something special, and *that* didn't happen every day.

With a sigh, she tilted her drink to her lips and almost poured the rest of the contents down her face. Blaze sat across from her at the table. Sputtering, she wiped her chin. "Give a warning next time." She sat the glass down, looking to see if she spilled any down her shirt.

"Sorry." He smirked, his eyes searching hers.

"No, you're not." Jill also watched him closely. "What happened to your face?" He had a cut above his eyebrow with faded bruising under his eye.

"Your mate." His tone was flat, but respect shimmered in his eyes.

This time Jill smirked. "Guess it's a good thing you heal fast." When he didn't respond, she narrowed her eyes. "So, that thing you did to me is how you got your name?"

He cocked his eyebrow with a nod, but remained silent.

"Listen, I was just being a smartass. I didn't mean to offend you," Jill said, uncomfortable under his scrutiny. "I've been hanging around Sid and Jared too long. It wasn't even a good smartass remark really. About your name I mean."

A smile finally tilted his lips, but he still remained silent.

Jill huffed. "So did you just come in here to stare at me and make me nervous, or is there another reason?"

"I like you." His smile disappeared slowly. "I don't usually like anyone."

"Ah, okay. That's a good thing... I think." Jill grinned and then gazed at his huge arms. "So do any of those tattoos have meaning?" She figured getting away from the subject of him liking her was safe. At least he liked her; she didn't need this big guy as an enemy.

He only nodded.

Jill rolled her eyes. Looked like she would be doing all the talking. "I want to get a tattoo, but I don't like pain. Did they hurt bad?"

He shook his head this time.

Well crap. "You don't like to talk much, do you?"

Before he could answer, Sid walked in. "What the fuck are you doing in my kitchen?"

Blaze didn't move, didn't even look at Sid, but continued to stare at Jill. Her eyes went back and forth, finally stopping on Blaze. She leaned slightly across the table to whisper to him. "I think he's talking to you."

"He knows who I'm talking to." Sid growled, slamming his hand on the table as he hovered over Blaze.

A different look shadowed Blaze's eyes as he slowly pushed his seat back with his legs, then just as slowly stood to face Sid.

"Guys." Jill also stood, wondering how to diffuse the situation.

"Looks like you and the doc had words." He stared at his eye. "Didn't learn the lesson the doc beat into you?" Sid stood nose to nose with Blaze.

"What is your problem?" Blaze didn't back away an inch.

Jill wedged herself between them, which was no easy feat. "Yes, he learned his lesson." She told Sid, getting between them. She attempted to push them apart. It didn't work. "And he has no problem," she told Blaze.

Blaze grabbed her arms, picking her up and moving her safely away, all the while staring at Sid. "Oh, he has a problem." Blaze stopped Jill with his arm when she started back between them. "And I'm about ready to take care of it."

"Oh, for the love of…" Jill threw her hands up, using her power to separate the two men. She tried not to grin when Blaze stopped his stare down with Sid to look at her in surprise. "Yeah, I got moves too."

"Jill, stay out of this," Sid hissed, digging his feet in against her power.

"No," she replied, her Pepsi and crackers churning in her stomach. "I'm sick of you guys always fighting."

"Who's fighting?" Steve walked in stopping beside Jill and stared at

Sid and Blaze who were glaring at each other.

"Isn't it obvious?" Jill rolled her eyes, her power slipping away. "You think you can stop asking stupid questions and help me before they kill each other?"

"Uh, no." Steve shook his head with a snort. "I've stayed alive this long by not getting between huge men, and those are two big sons a bitches." He thumbed over his shoulder at Sid and Blaze.

Jill dropped her arms in defeat, then threw them up in the air. "Go ahead and kill each other then." She walked backward, slamming down into a chair, crossing her legs and arms. "Men. You guys are so full of yourselves, thinking nothing of anyone but yourselves. I'm sick and just used every ounce of energy I had keeping you apart, and all for what? For you guys to prove who has the bigger cock?"

"Oh, God." Steve and Sid moaned at the same time.

"What?" Jill glared at them. "It's true. And for one, I'm sick and tired of it. So go ahead, maybe one of you will kill the other and then there will be one less cock contest around this damn place."

"Okay, first off there is no such thing as a cock contest." Steve actually blushed. "And please stop saying the word cock. It makes me damn uncomfortable."

"Why, 'cause I'm a girl?" Jill figured as long as she continued, Sid and Blaze weren't killing each other. She tilted her head staring directly at Steve. "Cock. Cock. Cooooccccckkkk!"

Sid and Blaze burst out laughing as Steve glared at Jill. "You aren't right."

"Ha! Looks who's talking." Jill tossed back before looking at Sid and Blaze, who didn't look like they wanted to kill each other anymore. Cock had many benefits it seemed. "Sid, can you please see if you can fix me something to eat that I don't want to throw up? Maybe something easy on the stomach? So far I've held Pepsi and crackers down."

Frowning, Sid looked concerned, taking a moment to study her. Then turning, he headed deeper into the kitchen and ignored Blaze, which was Jill's plan. Though she seriously doubted she could eat anything since her stomach was churning and burning.

"So, you still mad at me?" Steve eyed Jill and sat across from her, offering a 'you love me and know it' look. Blaze also sat down, his eyes taking in everything.

Jill wrinkled her nose at him and then sighed. "I guess not, but I was going to tell him."

"Sure you were," Steve replied while giving her the 'I call bullshit' look. "Did you take the pregnancy test?"

Shaking her head, she glanced over at Blaze, then quickly away when their eyes met. "No. Slade said there was no reason to."

Nodding, Steve turned to look at Blaze. "So, have you been here long enough to tell us why you're an ex-Warrior?" When Blaze didn't answer, Steve and Jill shared a look. "Guess not."

"He isn't a talker," Jill added, hiding her eagerness to hear the scoop on Blaze.

Sid set a bowl of rice down in front of her, along with a banana. "Eat slowly." He sat down at the table with a cup of coffee. "Where's the doc?"

Jill forked at the rice letting it cool, not really wanting to put it in her mouth. She knew she had to since Sid made it. "He went to the hospital." She didn't want to add with her blood, because honestly, she didn't want to think about what he might find.

"What happened in Sloan's office?" Sid kept up his interrogation, his eyes going back and forth between Jill and Blaze.

Great, here we go again. "I just got lightheaded." Jill shrugged, continuing to fork her rice. "No big deal."

"Don't make me feed it to you," Sid warned, watching her play with the food. "You need to eat."

She scowled at him. "I'm letting it cool, Dad."

Sid grinned and sipped his coffee, his eyes going to Blaze. "So, what's your story?"

"I'm here to help Jax," Blaze answered to Jill's surprise. "The end."

Sid cocked an eyebrow over his coffee cup, but didn't comment further. Jill watched the steam rolling off Sid's coffee, her eyes going to Blaze. "Can you set things on fire?"

Blaze had been staring off, but his eyes slammed into hers. "Yes."

"Give me a lighter and so can I." Steve looked at Blaze, unimpressed. "So is that why you got thrown out of the VC because you're a fire bug? I knew it had to be something. No one just walks."

Jill watched a strange emotion cross Blaze's face, before he turned to stare at Steve. Jill knew that stare. She watched his eyes swirl as they took a dark golden hue. Sitting back in her chair, a half-grin on her face, she watched both Blaze and Steve.

"They have help for people like that," Steve replied, being his helpful self. "What do they call people who set fires? Dammit, it's right on the tip of my tongue."

Jill couldn't help but smile as Steve shifted uncomfortably in his seat, a bead of sweat sliding down his forehead.

"Pyromaniac," Blaze replied, his voice even as his eyes swirled crazily.

Steve snapped his fingers. "That's it, pyromaniac. Damn man, you need to get help for that. Sloan will be *pissssed* if you…" Steve reached across the table to grab Jill's napkin. "Shit, it's hot in here. Are you hot? I'm burning up."

Jill watched Steve swipe the sweat off his face with the napkin; she tried not to laugh.

"I hope to hell I'm not catching what you have." Sweat just poured off him. "But that's impossible since I'm full blood and don't get sick."

Glancing at Sid, she saw that he was watching Blaze and Steve closely, with a very interested expression on his face as well as a half-grin.

Fanning himself with the napkin, Steve's face was red. Jill turned to tell Blaze to stop, like he would even listen to her, and saw Blaze's golden eyes shift to a red glaze. Okay, that was creepy as hell.

"Ah…" Jill started to give Steve a warning, but it was too late. The napkin in Steve's hand burst into flames.

Steve screamed, throwing the napkin before pushing back so hard from the table he and the chair fell to the floor. As fast as Steve hit the ground, he popped back up, pointing at the smoking ashes that was the napkin, then pointed to Blaze. "Holy shit!" Steve looked at his fingers, wiggling them in front of his face then back to Blaze. "Hence the name."

Blaze nodded, his eyes back to normal in a flash. "Easier to show, than tell."

"Maybe for you," Steve grumbled, wiping the sweat from his face, then fanning his shirt. "Can you make someone burst into flames like you did that napkin?"

"Yes." Blaze glanced at Sid, then back to Steve. "But it smells, so I usually don't."

"Ah…it smells," Steve mocked, throwing up his hands. "Well, good thing for me."

"Pretty impressive." Sid took a drink of his coffee, his stare still intense. "Now I know where I've heard that name."

Tension thickened in the room practically smothering Jill. "You know him?" she asked Sid, but wished she hadn't when Blaze stood quickly.

"Not personally," Sid replied, his relaxed posture didn't reach his eyes. He and Blaze had one hell of a staring contest going on.

"Meaning?" Steve ventured to ask.

"Meaning he needs to keep his mouth shut." Blaze's body stiffened, his hands balling into fists.

"Okaaay." Steve took two steps back to stay out of the way of the shitstorm brewing.

A humorless smile spread on Sid's face. Taking a long, final drink of his coffee, he gently set the cup down and stood. "You man enough to see that happen?"

Standing with a huff, Jill slammed her hands on the table. She opened her mouth to start saying cock again, but the kitchen door opened, stopping her. Pam stumbled in. Her face unusually pale, she held onto the door long enough to steady herself.

"Hey guys." Her voice sounded hoarse and weak.

"Pam, you okay?" Jill frowned, watching her closely, the burning in her stomach rising to meet her heart that just dropped.

Pam nodded and took two steps before her knees buckled.

"Sid!" Jill yelled out the warning, but Sid was already there to catch Pam.

"Get Duncan and Slade, now!" Sid ordered loudly. Steve ran out the door to do just that. "Pam! Come on, girl, you can't do this shit to me again."

Jill ran around them, grabbed a clean cloth, wet it with cold water, and brought it to Sid.

"Shit!" Sid laid Pam down, putting his large hand behind her head to cushion it from the hard floor. "Where in the fuck is Duncan?"

Jill grabbed her phone calling Slade, but it went straight to voice mail. She just hoped he was on the phone with Steve, but just in case, she texted him.

"I'm okay." Pam coughed. When she tried to sit up, Sid stopped her.

"Oh, hell no." Sid carefully pushed her back down. "You're staying right there until Duncan and Slade get here. How in the hell could you do this to me again, Pam?"

"I promise not to sneeze," she teased weakly.

"Yeah, well, that doesn't mean shit since there's no baby to shoot out now, is there?" Sid's eyes widened. "Or is there?"

"I'm not pregnant." Pam snorted, closing her eyes. "I've been sick the past week and haven't been able to keep anything down. I was coming in here to see if there were crackers or something."

Sid and Jill shared a look. "Have you been able to feed?" Jill asked from her kneeling position next to Pam.

"I feed, but it comes back up." Pam opened her eyes. "Why?"

Jill didn't answer as a feeling of despair so strong filled her, knocking her back on her ass.

"Don't you be passing out!" Sid ordered Jill, as if he had any control over her passing out or not. Blaze actually walked to stand beside her, ready to catch her just in case.

"I'm fine." Her eyes met Pam's, and in that moment, something passed between them.

"You're doing the same thing?" Pam asked, her voice trembling in fear she was unable to hide.

Nodding, Jill didn't say anything because she knew she wouldn't be able to hide her own fear.

# CHAPTER 5

Jill moved out of the way with Blaze's help when Duncan ran into the kitchen with Steve hot on his heels.

"What's wrong, babe?" Duncan slid to his knees beside her. "What happened?"

"I'm okay now." Pam tried to smile up at him, but failed miserably. "I just got a little lightheaded."

"Where's Daniel?" Duncan looked around, but held tightly to her hand.

"He's with Katrina. I came down here for something to eat." Pam tried to sit up, but Duncan wouldn't let her.

"Where in the hell is Slade?" Duncan growled, his eyes finding Jill.

"I'm right here." Slade walked in, his eyes finding Jill right away. "What happened?"

Again Jill and Pam glanced at each other. "She's sick," Jill answered. "Like me."

Jill could never remember seeing Slade look so bleak when she answered him, his eyes darting away from her. Okay, that was very telling. This was not good. He knew something and that something was not good news.

"When did this start?" Slade took off his leather jacket as he replaced Sid and knelt next to Pam.

"I haven't been feeling very well for a few weeks. Real run down." Pam glanced at Duncan. "I didn't say anything because I didn't think it was anything."

"You should have told me." Duncan's voice was gentle, edged with worry.

"You guys have been so busy with the funerals and I just didn't feel it was important. Daniel has his days and nights messed up again so I thought I was just worn down, but then…" She looked over at Jill.

"But then what?" Duncan demanded.

"She can't keep blood down," Jill answered for her. Everyone looked at her, except for Duncan who continued to stare at Pam until he finally looked over at Slade.

"What does this mean?" Duncan's face indicated he was at a loss and wasn't happy about it.

"I don't know yet." Slade frowned without looking Duncan in the eye. His focus stayed on Pam.

Jill knew Slade had an idea of the problem. His inability to keep eye contact with her was a dead giveaway. Slade always made eye contact…always.

"But I do need to take some of her blood." Slade stood. "Can you get her to my office?"

Duncan's answer was to pick Pam up carefully. "I can walk now." Pam wrapped her arms around Duncan's neck.

"No, you can't." Duncan ignored her protests, his love evident in the way he held her.

Jill watched Duncan carry Pam out the door, her eyes going to Slade, not knowing if she should stay or go. "Do you need help?" she asked, at a loss.

"No." Slade glanced at everyone before his eyes came back to hers. "I thought I told you to rest."

"I wanted to see if some crackers would help my stomach," she answered. "And Sid fixed me some rice."

"Which she didn't eat," Sid told him and didn't look like he regretted doing it one bit.

"But I did eat some crackers and kept them down." Jill crossed her arms around her stomach, trying to calm the churning, hoping to keep her statement of keeping it down true.

"Try to eat a little more if you can and I'll be back as soon as I finish with Pam." Slade walked over, placed a kiss on the top of her head, and then turned and walked out of the kitchen.

Jill watched the door shut behind him before looking at Sid and Steve, who had busied themselves with something other than watching her and Slade's little moment. Blaze, on the other hand, had sat back down and was staring at her. Before she could say anything to Blaze, because in all honesty his quiet staring was really starting to unnerve her, Sid stepped into her line of vision.

"Slade is not going to let anything happen to you." Sid stared down at her. "So get that worried look off your face and eat some rice. I just warmed it up for you."

With a small smile, Jill nodded and headed toward her seat at the table. The warm steaming bowl of rice looked disgusting at the moment. Steve sat down across from her and openly stared. His face pinched in concern.

"You're going to be okay, Jill," Steve said, as if by him just saying those words it was a done deal. "We're vampires. Nothing can bring us down, right?"

Jill nodded, her tongue feeling like it was glued to the roof of her mouth. "Right," she replied, but her heart told her she was far from right.

******

Slade opened the drawer to his medical cabinet and noticed his hands shaking. He stopped and stared at them as Duncan and Pam talked softly behind him. Closing his eyes, he balled his hands into fists, trying to get a grip on his emotions. Out of every horror he had faced in his thousands of years, nothing had terrified him more than the news he had received today.

"Hey," Duncan called out. "You going to take her blood or what?"

Slade's eyes opened. A tick pulsated in his jaw from clamping his mouth shut tightly against the bellow of rage he felt. Slowly, he un-fisted his hands, grabbed what he needed and moved his jaw back and forth. No need to alarm Pam until he had more answers.

Going through the motions of taking Pam's blood, Slade felt Duncan probing his thoughts, but he shut them off with a warning to wait until they were alone. Duncan backed off and focused on Pam.

Once the three vials of blood were taken and safely in the envelopes, he turned to them both. "I'll take these to the hospital and let you know the results as soon as I know anything."

Pam nodded, but her eyes searched his. "It's not good, is it?"

Slade didn't know what to say, because she was right. It wasn't good…for any of them. "You need to rest, Pam. Have Katrina help with Daniel when Duncan's not around. You need to preserve your energy and try to eat, but only a little bland food. Don't feed until I tell you."

Watching them leave the office, Duncan threw Slade an 'I'll be back' look over Pam's head. Once alone, Slade glanced down at the envelopes containing Pam's blood. Bleak rage consumed him. Undeterred, he grabbed the envelopes, headed out of his office and back to the kitchen. But seeing Jill gone, and Sid telling him she went up to their room to rest, Slade hurried to Sloan's office.

Finding Sloan alone, he knew by the angry expression on Sloan's face the news he was about to hear was not good.

"They cannot refuse this request." Slade's control slipped a little. He placed the envelopes on Sloan's desk in fear of breaking the vials inside. Without Sloan telling him, Slade knew they had been refused.

"They can and they have." Sloan watched Slade closely, waiting for the blow up. "I've called everyone in here, but you need to keep calm, Slade. We need you focused because you may be their only hope."

Eyes blackening in rage, Slade's chest heaved as a sneer curved his lips. His eyes looked around for something to smash, but Sloan's words reached part of his brain that was still reasonable. He did have to get a grip. Jill's life depended on it, not to mention every manmade half-breed out there. "I don't want Jill here. I want to tell her alone."

Sloan nodded, picking up his phone. After he finished, he looked up at Slade. "Adam hasn't shown any symptoms, has he?"

Slade shook his head. "Not that I know of."

"I told Adam the meeting was cancelled, as well as Steve, because Steve has a big mouth." Sloan leaned back in his chair, staring at Slade. "We'll figure this out. She'll be fine."

But at what cost? The silent question hovered between the Warriors while they waited for everyone.

******

Jill lay on the bed with her eyes closed, but her mind racing. Sitting up, she grabbed the bridal magazine laying next to her. Nicole, Tessa, and Pam were driving her crazy with all the wedding hoopla. She'd be happy to grab a minister, head in the woods behind her old house, and marry Slade beneath the trees she was so fond of. But ever since Slade set a date, which was in three weeks, the women had been driving her nuts. So in order to get them off her back, she had given them the go ahead to set up everything. They were calling themselves the Warrior Wedding Planners and even talked about going into business. Thumbing through the magazine, Jill grinned at the thought.

Her stomach grumbled and her throat tightened with thirst, thirst for Slade's blood. Swallowing hard, she continued to look through the magazine trying to ignore the uncomfortable feeling until her door flew open.

"Hey." Steve and Adam walked into her and Slade's room.

"Hey," she replied, tossing the magazine. "And you better watch bursting into the room like that. You've already caught Slade naked once and he wasn't too happy about it."

"Seeing Slade and his, well you know, wasn't very pleasant." Steve frowned. "It made me downright depressed."

Adam glared over at Steve. "Dude, are you gay?"

"No, I'm not," Steve replied, then looked at Jill. "But if I were, I sure would be giving you a run for your money, 'cause I mean… whoa."

"You are messed up, man." Adam shook his head.

"Yeah, well, you didn't see what I saw." Steve snuck a grin at Jill. "So what do you think is going on?"

"Where?" Jill asked, scooting back to lean against the headboard.

Adam and Steve glanced at each other. "You didn't get the text from Sloan?" Adam asked.

Grabbing her phone to double check, she shook her head. "No."

Steve frowned. "We both received a text saying the meeting was cancelled."

"I didn't even get one about a meeting. Oh, well, maybe something came up and he didn't get around to texting everyone," Jill leaned her head back, tired.

"Sloan doesn't individually text everyone…duh." Steve hopped on the bed, making himself comfortable. "Group messaging is the thing now, Jill. Get with the program."

Okay, that woke her up. Steve was right for once. "Then why was I left off?" She sat up and looked at Adam.

"Not sure." Adam stood against the wall, arms crossed. "But I think we should go find out because obviously this has to do with us since we saw Jared, Damon, and Jax heading into an already full office for a meeting you weren't even invited to and we were uninvited."

Steve jumped up from the bed, a huge smile on his excited face. "So how we going to do this?"

"Ah, walk into Sloan's office." Jill slowly clambered off the bed.

"Ah, no." Steve headed toward the door. "Obviously they don't want us there so we need to do this the Warrior way."

Jill didn't know if she was up for the Warrior way at that moment, but no way in hell would she admit that, and Steve was right. The Warriors wouldn't say a word if they showed up.

Steve snapped his fingers. "I've got a plan."

"No," both Jill and Adam said at the same time.

"What do you mean, no? I haven't even told you yet." Steve threw his hands out, but then looked up at the ceiling and pointed. "Sloan has one of those above his desk."

Jill and Adam looked to where he was pointing. It was an air vent. "You're crazy." Jill's eyes widened. "That will never work. They'd hear us before we got close enough."

Steve thought for a minute. "True. We are dealing with Warriors who can hear a mouse fart, but we all know how these meetings go. Everyone talking at once, Sid throwing in jokes after anyone talks. It's never quiet and they will be distracted because this meeting seems to be pretty serious business."

Sighing, Jill didn't respond as she left the room.

"Come on, Jill," Steve called out after her. "I've always wanted to do that and this is our chance. It will work."

"A mouse fart?" Adam gave him a sideways look as he passed

Steve to follow Jill.

"Hey, they get gas," Steve grumbled, following. "Come on, guys. I even know where to get in. We can do this."

# CHAPTER 6

Jill walked straight up to Sloan's door, but stopped. She knew this room was soundproof, but as Steve pointed out, they were also Warriors. Kneeling down, she scooted sideways next to the door and pressed her ear against it.

"Oh, and this is a better idea than mine." Steve snorted with a pout. "This is—"

"Shush." Jill smacked his leg.

Adam and Steve planted themselves above Jill putting their ears to the door. "This is stupid," Steve whispered. "My plan was sooo much better."

Jill pinched his leg hard, but didn't say anything. The first voice she heard was Slade. His voice was harsh and filled with an anger that made her hold her breath.

"I don't care what they say." Slade's voice reached their ears as they eavesdropped through the door. "If it comes down to it, I will change her and no one will stop me."

"Then you will lose everything." Concern laced Sloan's words. "Are you prepared for that?"

Jill glanced up at Adam, who still had his ear pressed against the door, but was staring down at her.

Something blew air on her fingers making Jill look down at her hand. Her fingers were halfway under the door. Figuring it was just someone passing the door creating a flow of air, she ignored it, until it happened again. But this time, it sounded like something was sniffing. With a frown, she eased her face down to the floor to look under the door. What she saw surprised her. Between two furry paws was a large black nose. Popping back up, Jill's eyes widened, wondering who got a dog. Before she could say anything, a loud growl came from under the door and it swung open.

Steve and Adam fell through the open doorway past the biggest, meanest looking dog Jill had ever seen with Jax standing behind it. Jill back peddled as the dog leaped out the door toward her. Her only thought was to keep the huge beast off her. She rolled back on her elbows catching the beast in mid leap with her feet and tossing it over her head. Standing quickly, she turned to see the animal land gracefully and shift before her shocked eyes into a naked man, who looked almost as wild as the beast. His hair was a dirty blonde with raven streaks, his eyes a mixture of wildness and calm control. It was a mind-blowing contrast.

He stood slowly, clearly not embarrassed by his nakedness. Jill's eyes stayed on his, waiting for the next threat, but Slade was in front of her taking any threat out of the picture.

"What in the fuck are you three doing?" Sloan walked out, casting a hard stare at Adam, Steve, and Jill.

None of them were brave enough to answer. Instead, they remained silent looking guilty as hell.

Jill peeked around Slade to the man who was now grabbing clothes from Jax and putting them on. His eyes met hers and he grinned at her with a wink. Glancing away quickly, she hoped Slade hadn't seen that, but his deep growl dashed her hopes.

"Get your asses in here," Sloan ordered, stomping into his office to his desk.

"Told you this was a stupid idea." Steve glared at Jill before following Sloan and the other Warriors into the office. "We would have never been caught with my idea."

Slade took her hand to lead her into the office.

"Nice move, shorty." The man, now fully dressed stopped in front of Jill.

"Never threaten her again." Slade sneered, his grip on her hand tightened.

The man held up his hands, a crooked grin on his face. "Hey, sorry, man. But where I come from threats are everywhere, even with pretty—"

Blaze who had been standing on the sideline walked up and pushed the man toward the office, coming between Slade and him. "They also don't know when to shut the fuck up where he comes from."

Glancing up at Slade, she watched the tick in his jaw and his eyes were dark with anger. Without looking down at her, he pulled her into the office slamming the door behind them, then let go of her hand.

"So much for telling her alone." Sloan's eyes narrowed on the three who weren't supposed to be there. "And just fair warning, you are on report."

"What?" Jill frowned. "Why?"

"Are you seriously asking me why?" Sloan's voice rose slightly. Before Jill could say anything, he continued. "You were left out of this meeting for a reason. It is a serious offense to eavesdrop on confidential VC matters."

"VC matters that have to do with me," Jill shot back with as much respect as she could muster. "And them." She pointed to Adam and Steve. Steve gave her a 'leave me out of your bitchfest' look.

"Jill." Slade's voice was stern.

"What?" she shot back. "Were you or were you not discussing me?"

When no one answered, Jill crossed her arms waiting.

"I for one—" Steve cleared his throat.

"You were left out because you have a big mouth." Sloan cut Steve off with a warning glance.

"Good to know." Steve took a step back with a nod of relief.

"And me?" Adam's deep voice rang out.

Sloan and Slade looked at each other for a spit second. "I'm not sure if this is going to have anything to do with you or not yet."

"For shit's sake." The man who Jill had never seen before in her life, took a step forward. "Tell her and get it over with. She has a right to know."

Jill's eyes opened in surprise. "He knows?" Betrayal swirled in her gut. With narrowed eyes, she looked up at Slade. "Somebody I've never met before in my life knows whatever in the hell you are trying to hide from me. Who in the hell are you anyway?"

Having eyes for no one other than Slade, she had to give this guy credit. He was good looking and had a weird attraction vibe going for him, especially when he smiled, which he did directly at her. "Hunter Foster," he said and ended with another wink.

"Choo...choo." Sid sighed, his eyebrows raised as he looked from Hunter to Slade then back to Hunter.

Hunter opened his mouth to say something, but Slade's fist closed it. Hunter's head snapped back fast as he wiped the blood from his mouth. "Chill out, man." Hunter worked his neck. "I'm not out for your lady, just being friendly."

"I'd say maybe, just maybe you tone down that friendliness when dealing with our mates unless you want the Slade Train to make another stop on your face," Jared said with a shake of his head.

Hunter nodded, looking Slade up and down. "Noted." He grinned, working his jaw back and forth. "But if that was my lady, I sure as hell wouldn't be keeping anything from her."

Jared looked at Sid. "They never learn."

"Hunter." Jax shook his head at him in warning.

"Keeping what from me?" Jill ignored everyone, looking into every Warrior's eyes until they stopped on Slade.

"You know nothing." Slade growled at Hunter.

"I'm part wolf and I smell death on her." Hunter's easy banter disappeared, seriousness straightened his features and filled the room with tension. "And I say it's not far off, so I would stop—"

It took every Warrior in the room to separate the Warrior and the wolf, except Jill, who stood back watching everything move as if in slow motion. She was dying? Watching the Warriors all bunched-up and wrestling around, a surge of anger overpowered her. The shaking started as she walked toward them. Her arms outstretched as power radiated from her. Without thought to what she was doing, each Warrior she aimed her hands at went flying, until there was only Slade and Hunter left. Two tears ran down her face, one clear and one blood red.

******

A film of rage shadowed everything inside Slade. Just hearing the word death and Jill in the same sentence was enough to send him over the edge. All he wanted to do was take out the person who dared speak the sentence. Power enveloped him as he rolled around, with Warriors pulling at him and the man underneath him protecting himself. Soon the weight on his back lightened and he was forcibly yanked away and rolling across the floor. His rage disappeared at the ravaged face of Jill standing over him.

"Jill." Slade tried to stand, but she used her power to keep him plastered on the floor. "You need to stop. You need to…"

"I need to do nothing." Jill glared down at him. "But you need to tell me what in the hell is going on because honestly, I'm about to lose it."

Slade felt her power weakening and it worried him. Managing to stand against her power, he took two steps, grabbed her arms and put them down to her side. With one hand, he wiped the tears off her face. "I won't let anything happen to you." Truth and promise radiated with every syllable.

Looking toward Duncan, Jill's lip quivered as she looked back up at Slade. "Is Pam…?"

"No one is going to fucking die." Slade pulled her into his arms, not caring that everyone was in the room staring at them. Glancing at Damon, he nodded toward the chair. Damon carried the chair over for Jill, who gratefully sank into it.

"Shouldn't Pam be here?" Jill frowned up at Slade.

Slade put his hand on Jill's shoulder, his thumb rubbing back and forth. His eyes met Duncan's whose pain reflected his own. No Warrior wanted to see their mate in danger and that was exactly what was happening, but it wasn't against anything they could physically fight. That was killing him the most.

"It's up to you," Slade told Duncan, waiting for his answer, but when Duncan wordlessly shook his head, Slade nodded then looked down at Jill. "I wanted to tell you this alone."

"Obviously this isn't just about me so I'd rather you just tell me now," Jill replied, her voice quivering at the end. She cleared her throat trying to hide the fear in her voice, and he loved her even more for it.

"I took Jill's blood samples to the hospital," Slade began, his fingers tightening on her shoulder. "Dr. Vaughn, who is a highly acclaimed hematologist…"

"Is he going to start talking doctor?" Sid whispered to Jared.

Slade glared at them both. "He studies blood."

"I knew that." Jared winked at Jill who was half-smiling up at him.

"Bullshit." Sid snorted.

Slade tried to keep his shit together and knew that Sid and Jared were trying to lighten the dark mood, but he was on a dangerous spiral and honestly didn't know if he could take much more. Anything could set him off and he knew it. Jill was slowly dying and until he had a definite answer on how to save her, he was on the edge of destruction. Anyone in his way was in grave danger. Gazing down at Jill, he saw her attention was back on him. She knew him well. Well enough to know he was close to losing it.

"What did the doctor find?" Jill's voice was strong, but her eyes showed the fear she couldn't hide, and it killed him.

"Your human leukocytes are attacking and destroying—"

"You already lost me," Jill said before Sid or Jared could say anything.

Slade kneeled down in front of her. "Whatever they gave you…" he then glanced at Duncan and Adam, "…gave all of you is failing. The human body is a force to be reckoned with and is finding a way to fight against what's foreign in your body, which is the serum you were given."

"But that was so long ago." Jill said, her forehead wrinkled in confusion. "Why now?"

"That's something I can't answer." Those words were bitter on his tongue. "But the human body is constantly trying to find ways to fight off disease, infections, or anything foreign. You all were given a manmade drug, which we're still trying to decipher exactly what it contained. Without knowing what the serum consists of, we don't know what to look for to reverse this process, or if there is a way to reverse it."

"Okay, so what you're saying is my…" Jill frowned. "What did you call them?"

"Leukocytes, which is your white blood cells that seek out and fight off disease-causing organisms or substances." Slade's fist tightened in anger, but he kept his voice calm.

"So my body is fighting for me to be human again." Jill's voice cracked.

"In a sense, yes." Slade looked away from her as his mind bellowed for him to lie, but his loyalty to her refused. She deserved the truth, but the truth was enough to bring him to his knees, which was exactly where he was—on his knees in front of the woman he loved more than his own life.

Her small hand touched his cheek bringing his face to hers. "But I don't want to be human," she whispered for his ears only, but everyone in the room heard her words.

Slade felt her pain and fear in each word. His eyes searched hers and without him saying another word, understanding flashed across her face.

"I won't be human, will I?" Jill didn't take her eyes off him as they opened wider with realization. "But I won't be a half-breed either. Hunter's right. I'm dying, aren't I?"

Head bowed for a split second, the tick in Slade's jaw beat fast and hard as he slammed his eyes shut, getting himself under control. With a fluid motion, he swept her into his arms and stood. "No, you are not going to die." His voice rose with each word as he turned toward Sloan. "I want a meeting with whatever asshole I need to meet with in the human government."

Sloan nodded, silent for once.

"Go take care of Pam and I will be up there in a half an hour, but do not under any circumstance let her feed from you." Slade ordered Duncan before turning to Adam. "I need you in my office to take blood." After Adam nodded, Slade turned and walked out the door, holding Jill close.

For the first time, every Warrior in Sloan's office was silent as the grim reality of what was happening shadowed their world.

# CHAPTER 7

Caroline sat on the rotting roof of her new house, a notepad in her hand wondering if this was indeed going to trump Rod and be the biggest mistake she had ever made in her life. Looking around the property, all she saw was thick lush woods. It was absolutely beautiful. So what if the house was about to fall apart around her, she could always pitch a tent.

Lana and her parents thought she was nuts and did everything in their power to talk her out of the purchase, but nothing they said could sway her. She wanted this property and it was now hers.

While going through a very short time of feeling sorry for herself, she had watched a lot of television and got hooked on shows about flipping houses. Buying beautiful properties that needed loving care, fixing them up then reselling them sounded perfect. At this point, she didn't know what she wanted to do after flipping it, but as her eyes scanned over her backyard, she knew this was her forever home in all its peeling paint and rotting roof glory. She felt it the moment she pulled into the driveway the first time. It was her place to do what she wanted.

So what if she had to do it alone. She could do this without the help of a man, well except a roofer who was due there any minute. She was done with men in so many ways. Her dad was the only male she would ever trust.

Running her tongue along her lips, her stomach tightened as her mind drifted to the kiss she shared with Jax. No man had ever kissed her that way and what upset her most was no man probably would. He was one of the main reasons she got addicted to all the home improvement shows because she never left the house after that kiss. She just stayed in and watched television eating Grater's Double Chocolate Chip Ice Cream out of the container with the biggest spoon she could find. It would totally be his fault if she had made the biggest mistake in her life buying the rundown farmhouse and not being able to fit in her clothes, the ass. It felt damn good blaming him, which she did just in spite. Not one phone call, text or anything from him since the kiss. She had even stopped going to see Lana hoping to get a peek at him. It didn't take her long to get the hint, so she turned her fascination with the Warrior into anger, ice cream, and home improvement.

"Screw him," she whispered to herself, and then smiled, realizing the power of those words. "Screw him!" she said louder, with more force.

"What in the hell are you doing up there?" A familiar voice called from the ground. "And who the fuck do you want to screw?"

Caroline jumped, her phone flying out of her hand. She scrambled to catch it, but it hit the roof and plunged toward the ground. Sliding on her butt as quick as she could, she was too late. It went over the edge and into the hand of a man who wasn't the roofer.

She sighed in relief that her phone wasn't smashed on the ground, but frowned at the man who saved it. "What are you doing here?"

"I asked you first." His frown was fierce as he glared up at her. "You're going to break your damn neck."

"I have a roofer coming and wanted to see how bad it was before he got here," she replied, wondering why she replied at all. "Not that it's any of your business. How did you even know where I was?"

"Lana. Now stay there and don't move," Jax ordered, pointing at her with her phone.

"Kill sister…check, and don't order me around." Caroline stood, putting her hands on her hips. Realizing she could never win a staring contest with Jax Wheeler, she turned away to walk to the front side of the roof where the ladder was.

"Caroline." The warning in his voice was clear, but she totally ignored him.

Not liking his tone of voice, she stomped her way up the roof without thinking. How dare he talk to her like that after ignoring her. "He can kiss my as…" She had been mumbling to herself before the roof gave way under her feet.

Jax shook his head as he watched her stomping on what he was sure was a rotten roof. She was saying something, but he wasn't paying attention. The sound of cracking filled his ears. In two strides, he was jumping onto the roof and reached her just as it opened up beneath her. Her scream cut short when he grabbed her, cleared the house, and landed in her front yard.

"Are you hurt?" He set her down, going instantly to his knees knowing one of her legs went through the roof.

"No." Her answer was breathless.

"What the hell happened?" Blaze followed by Hunter came rushing up to them.

"She decided to stomp around on a rotten roof." Jax knew his tone was harsh, but the thought of her falling through the roof scared the shit out of him.

"Not a very smart thing to do." Hunter glanced at the roof then back to her. "The whole place looks like it needs to be burned to the ground."

"Excuse me." Caroline gave him her best teacher stare. "And who are you?"

He gave her a sexy smile. "The name's Hunter Fos—"

His smile didn't move her in the least. "I didn't ask for your opinion, kid." Then she looked at Blaze who was trying to wipe the grin off his face. "And you?"

"Blaze." He cleared his throat.

She nodded to him. "Since he's too rude to introduce us, I'm Caroline, and it's nice to meet you…" She glanced at Hunter with a frown. "I think. And that's my home you're talking about burning down."

All three men glanced behind her to the shack she just called home. Jax frowned. "Your what?"

"My home." She smiled, looking at it as if seeing a palace instead of a falling-down, paint-peeling, termite-infested mess.

"I hope you can get your money back." Hunter winced when he heard a loud noise of boards falling from inside the house.

"And that kind of talk won't get you invited to dinner," Caroline snapped at him when she brushed past them, head held high to see what the noise was.

All three men watched her walk away, three pairs of eyes on her ass. Hunter took off after her. "Looks like I need to correct the pretty lady on the kid remark." His eyes remained fixed on the sway of her hips.

Jax grabbed him by the shirt tossing him back. "If you want to live, you'll shut the fuck up."

Hunter growled at him, but backed off at the look Jax tossed his way.

"You got a death wish?" Blaze stopped Hunter from following Jax. "Back off before I send you packing."

Jax heard every word spoken behind him, but ignored it as he followed Caroline into… He glanced at the sad little building and had a hard time calling it a house. He stopped just inside the door spotting Caroline staring up at the huge hole in her ceiling.

"Crap," Caroline cursed, staring up at the hole with her hands on her hips.

"Don't stand there," Jax ordered, expecting more danger to head her way.

Caroline turned to give him an evil frown. "This is your fault."

"My fault?" Jax glared back at her. "If this is the way you say thank you for saving you, you suck at it."

That stumped her for a second as she bit her lip. He could actually see her mind working. "Well, I wouldn't have needed saving if you wouldn't have made me mad."

"Ah, I see." Jax shook his head and folded his arms. This woman drove him absolutely insane and he wanted nothing more at that moment than to taste those frowning lips again. "So because I showed concern for your safety, you got mad and stomped on a disintegrating roof."

"What do you want, Jax?" Caroline quickly looked away from him and started cleaning up the mess in the middle of her kitchen floor. "I'm obviously busy and the roof guy is going to be here any minute. If you're here to tell me not to bother you anymore, well, I haven't been. I'm sorry I sent those two texts after you said to stay away…lesson learned."

Jax watched her, but kept a close eye on the ceiling above her head, ready for action if more boards and plaster decided to fall.

"And you didn't need to bring your buddies with you." She huffed picking up a large board and staggered as she moved it out of her way. "I got the hint."

Walking over, he nudged her out of the way grabbing the heavy boards before turning around to face her. "What in the hell are you talking about?" He glared down at her.

"Do you need your hearing checked?" Caroline ushered him out of her way continuing to clean up. "I thought vampires had excellent hearing."

"I heard you perfectly." Jax growled as he looked up to check the safety, but it didn't look safe at all. "I just don't understand what your problem is."

"No problem, Jax. Just tell me what you want." Caroline tossed a large piece of plaster, which landed directly on his foot. "Sorry." She muttered in a tone that clearly said she wasn't sorry at all.

Hurt crossed her face before she turned away twisting his gut. Dammit, he sucked when it came to women. He never said the right thing and more times than not, he ended up slapped or cursed. Frowning down at his plaster-covered shoes and pants, he sighed. "I am still trying to find Mika and need to know if you've talked to my sister."

With her back turned toward him, her shoulders stiffened. It was a minute before she answered.

"No, I haven't," she replied, her face blank of any emotion. "Is that all?"

Fuck no, that wasn't all, he wanted to shout, but didn't. He was trying to keep her safe, but she was too stubborn to see that. His brother would stop at nothing to harm anyone associated with him. Before he could say anything, Blaze stuck his head inside the front door.

"Some guy just pulled in." Blaze glanced up at the ceiling. "Damn."

Caroline walked past Jax without looking at him, straight past Blaze and out the door.

Jax started after her, but stopped when he spotted a sleeping bag in the corner of the room. Blaze followed his gaze.

"She cannot be sleeping in this place." Blaze frowned at the sleeping bag complete with pillow and a lantern.

"Son of a bitch." Jax headed toward the door, but his eyes stayed on her little sleeping place. She was crazy.

\*\*\*\*\*\*

Taking a deep breath as she stepped outside, Caroline tried to calm herself down. Damn that man to hell. Why did she fall for the assholes? Every single freaking time. *'Cause you're stupid, that's why.*

"Ms. Fitzpatrick?" a male voice interrupted her thoughts.

Caroline looked up to see an attractive man heading toward her, his smile friendly. He was well built, a little short for her liking... What in the hell was she doing? Was she that damn desperate that any good-looking guy smiling at her was a potential date to take her mind off the vampire whose kiss she couldn't forget?

"Yes, you must be Mr.... roofer guy." My God, she just sucked. "Sorry, I'm a little over my head here and can't remember anything."

He laughed; it was a pleasant laugh. "Just call me Gary."

"Well, Gary, I'm sure glad you're here." She turned to lead him to the house and ran smack into Jax who reached out to steady her from falling on her ass. Stepping back away from his broad chest, she looked up to see him glaring at the man following her. "If I hear anything from Alisha, I'll let you know," she dismissed him, but she should have known that no one dismissed Jax Wheeler if he didn't want to be dismissed.

When Jax didn't budge, she skirted around him, past Blaze and Hunter who also wore frowns. Hunter's was more like a smirk as he stared over her head at what she figured was Jax.

Gary, the roofer guy, was looking at the roof with narrowed eyes. "Well, I can tell you now before even climbing up there you have a lot of rotten wood to deal with."

"Kind of figured that out already, Gary." Caroline sighed when they stepped inside and she pointed toward the hole.

Gary paused under the hole and inspected it with a frown. "Anybody hurt?"

"No," Caroline replied, her gaze skimming past Jax, her face heating with a blush. "So what do you think this is going to cost me?"

Caroline was too busy scanning the ceiling to notice Gary eyeing her up and down, but Jax didn't miss it. "Can't say for sure yet." He gave her a friendly smile when she did look back to him. "Let me get up there and get some measurements."

"Oh, okay." Caroline returned his smile and watched him walk out. "He's a nice guy," she said, more to herself.

"He's a dick." Jax snorted, glaring at Gary's back.

"Yeah, well, you aren't paying him, now, are you?" she told him, following Gary.

"Neither will you," Jax vowed, taking one last glance at the sleeping bag before going outside.

"What?" Caroline heard Jax mumble something, but couldn't make it out.

Jax shook his head as he stared at her. "Are you staying here?"

Caroline's attention went from Gary, who was climbing the ladder, to Jax. "Yes, it's my home." She gave him a 'duh' look like she had seen so many of her kids give, then looked back at Gary who was walking on the roof. "Please be careful."

Gary tossed her a grin. "Don't worry. I've done this a million times."

"Bet he goes through." Hunter stood watching with what looked like a hopeful expression.

"What a mean thing to say," Caroline scolded.

"Oh, don't worry." Hunter grinned. "Jax will jump to his rescue."

"*That* I wouldn't bet on." Blaze chuckled, glancing at Jax.

"It's not safe for you to stay here." Jax ignored Hunter and Blaze.

Caroline ignored Jax other than rolling her eyes. As Gary climbed down the ladder, Caroline headed toward him. "So, how much is this going to hurt?" Caroline bit her lip glancing at his notebook that he had been writing in.

His eyes went straight to her lips before clearing his throat. "I need to get a quote written up before I give you an estimate. It's going to be costly. But I'll make sure we can work something out." He gave her a warm smile.

Jax's growl gained Gary and Caroline's attention. "She just needs an estimate for a roof and nothing more."

Caroline glared at Jax before turning back to Gary. "How long will that take?"

Gary was eyeing Jax cautiously before he answered. "I can have an estimate worked up by tomorrow afternoon." He looked behind him at the house. "Are you staying here?"

"Yes," Caroline answered without hesitation.

"Not alone," Jax added and before Caroline could say a word, he added, "We'll be waiting for the estimate."

Gary nodded. "Oh, okay." He stuck out his hand. "It was nice meeting you, Ms. Fitzpatrick."

"Thank you for coming out." Caroline shook his hand knowing her face was flaming red as she watched Gary glance at Jax before heading quickly to his truck.

"Who in the hell do you think you are?" Caroline all but shrieked as she smacked Jax on the arm.

"We'll go look for a tarp for the roof." Blaze grabbed Hunter, who was watching with a huge grin.

"Awe, just when it's getting good," Hunter moaned, but followed Blaze.

"Telling a man you don't know that you are staying here alone is not a smart move," Jax replied, his frown still firmly in place.

"He's a contactor." Caroline sighed, really not understanding the mixed signals Jax was sending her. "And I have a gun."

"He's a man," Jax replied as he walked past her. "And good."

Caroline turned to watch as Jax jumped up on the roof to help put the tarp Blaze and Hunter found to cover the hole. Watching them work Caroline was more confused than ever and wished he was still standing in front of her so she could smack him again.

# CHAPTER 8

Sloan slammed his phone down, picked it back up and slammed it again. "Stupid bastards." He hissed, rubbing his face. He was tired, so tired of everything. He once loved his position, but lately, he just wanted to walk. Being one of the few leaders who was against coming out to the human race, that phone call just proved why he had strongly felt that way. The fear and prejudice of most, especially the ones in power positions, pissed him off to the point if rogue vampires invaded their closed-minded space, he would look the other way. "Fuck!"

Picking up his phone again, he stared at it, feeling as if the walls were closing in on him. This news deserved to be told face-to-face instead of a text or a phone call. Standing, he stretched his tense muscles before heading out of his office. He stopped, looked around and stalled. He knew what this was going to lead to. Laughter came from the kitchen as he passed, but he didn't slow down. Silently, Sloan wondered when the last time was that he really laughed.

A grim frown slipped across his lips. He didn't have time to laugh. Hell, he didn't have time for anything, let alone laughing or enjoying even a second of anything.

"Jesus, I'm finally losing my fucking mind." Sloan shook his head in disgust. Knocking once on Slade's office door, he walked in.

Slade looked up from his desk. "Fuck!" Slade snarled, seeing Sloan's grim face.

"Yeah, fuck." Sloan closed the door behind him. "Just got off the phone with Dan Bentley, who is a spineless piece-of-shit and unfortunately, our representative with the human government."

"He human?" Slade asked, tossing his pen on the desk, rubbing his hand through his hair.

Sloan nodded. "It seems that there's an onslaught of requests coming in to change half-breeds." To follow was the information he dreaded. "All requests are being denied. The human government is afraid of vampires outnumbering humans."

"So they're playing God and deciding who lives and who doesn't." The truth of the statement sat heavily in the room. Palpable fury radiated off Slade. "I don't give a fuck what they deny. If it is a choice between her living or dying, I will change her and they can stick their denial up their asses."

"I figured you'd feel that way." Sloan sighed, not blaming Slade. "I'm sure Duncan will do the same thing, but know the risk you are taking."

"The only risk I see is losing Jill and that is not a risk I'm willing to take." Slade's eyes burned as he stared at Sloan, an unspoken message that was loud and clear passed between them.

"You know the consequences of changing someone without consent. We got away with it with Steve, but that was a whole different situation. It looks like what is happening with Pam and Jill is happening everywhere." Sloan wanted to make damn sure Slade knew exactly what was out of his control to stop from happening. "Not only will you be jailed and stripped of your VC Warrior status, but you will never be able to practice medicine, on human or vampire again."

"I know the fucking risks, Sloan." Slade growled, his voice raspy with emotion. "I have a wedding coming up in less than three weeks and if I don't fix this, I won't have a bride."

"Weddings get cancelled all the time." Sloan played the devil's advocate. He wanted to make damn sure he knew where Slade's head was because if he was going to fight for his Warriors, he needed to know without a doubt whatsoever in his own mind. The silence was deafening and he actually waited for Slade to attack, because he knew how much he loved Jill, but a calm façade shadowed Slade's features.

"Not mine." Slade's voice was deep with conviction.

******

Jill quietly backed away from Slade's door before turning around and walking away quickly. The hallway swam before her eyes as she stumbled away. The silence after Sloan said to cancel the wedding was enough for her to hear, but even if Slade had doubts, she would never allow him to put himself in a position to lose everything he had worked for, not for her.

Seeing Nicole and Tessa before they saw her, she ducked down another hallway and waited until they were gone. She didn't want to talk to anyone. No, that was a lie. Pulling her phone out, she shot off a text and waited. Relief settled over her as her phone dinged. Reading the text, she walked out of her hiding spot and headed out the front door, but not before she turned off her phone.

Walking toward one of the cars, she frowned checking her pockets, but she knew she didn't have the keys. "Crap." Spotting Adam's car, she grinned. "Ah, what the hell."

Jogging up to the car, she was happy it wasn't locked. Opening the door, she bent down and went to work. Within minutes, she had the car running. So he must be back to trusting her, his mistake. With a snort, Jill climbed in, backed up and pulled out of the driveway.

As she drove, her mind kept going back to Sloan and Slade's conversation, her stomach tightening with fear. Fear of death, fear of losing the only person she ever loved, and fear of watching him lose everything he ever worked for. She felt a full-blown panic attack coming on and fought it back.

After twenty minutes, she passed her old house and drove down a narrow dirt path. Seeing her brother's car, she smiled, instantly feeling better. He leaned against the driver's side door watching her with his familiar grin.

"Long time no see, stranger," Trevor teased. "Now that you're a big-time Warrior, you can't find time for us lowly humans?"

Okay, that hit her hard, but she kept the smile on her face. "Yeah, I have to pencil you in."

"You called me, remember." Trevor grabbed her in a hug and

ruffled her hair. "Smart ass."

Jill hugged him, not realizing how tight. "Missed you."

Trevor gasped for air. "Whoa, there, sis." He gently pushed at her. "You're squeezing me to death."

"Sorry." Jill pulled away then looked around. "Is the swing still up?"

"What's going on, Jill?" Trevor's smile slipped.

"What? I can't call my brother to hang for a little bit?" Jill didn't look at him; instead, she walked down the path she had walked more times than she could count. Things were different, yet comforting and the same. No, that wasn't right. Everything here was the same; she was different.

Trevor stepped next to her and placed his arm around her. Quietly, they made their way through the woods, Jill taking everything in. A sense of peace mixed with turmoil consumed her mind. Reaching the end of the path, which overlooked a large lake, Jill stepped to the edge.

"Water's up," she said absently, and then looked over at the old tree leaning over the calm water. "And there's the vine, still intact after all these years."

Trevor leaned up against a tree watching her closely. "Okay, Jill." He no longer wore a grin. "You're freaking me the hell out. What's going on?"

Jill pulled on the thick vine and sure enough, it held strong. With a sigh, she released it and sat down on a large boulder. "I'm sick, Trev."

"Whatever. You're a vampire." Trevor snorted, rolling his eyes, but when Jill didn't laugh he sat next to her.

"I'm half-vampire." Jill glanced at him with her mismatched eyes. "Long story short, whatever was in the serum they injected to change us is failing, and my body is fighting it off."

"You're shitting me." Trevor half-grinned, nudging her.

She nudged him back before looking back at him. "I wish I was."

Trevor stared at her for a minute then stood. "No!" He shook his head. "There has to be something they can do."

"It's not just me this is happening to." Jill sighed. "Sloan asked for permission for us to be changed to full blood, but it's been denied."

"Fuck them." Trevor hissed, his face paling as he truly realized how serious the situation was. "There's no way Slade is going to stand for that. Though I've only met him once, I saw how much he cares for you."

"He can't, Trevor." Standing, Jill glanced at the lake. "He could lose everything he worked for, plus be put in jail. I'm not going to let that happen."

"So you'll just die?" Trevor grabbed her arm. "There has to be another way."

Jill nodded before looking straight at him. "Do not say anything to Dad," Jill ordered. "I don't want him to worry."

Trevor remained silent, not agreeing or disagreeing.

"I mean it, Trevor," Jill warned. "Swear it."

"Okay." Trevor raised his hands in defeat.

"And Mom neither, not that she would care." Jill said and those the words hit her harder than usual. She would love to talk to her mom like a daughter should be able to. "But she would tell Dad and until things are grim, I don't want him to worry. His health is too important."

"She would care," Trevor replied. "And do you think that's fair to keep this from them?"

Jill thought about that for a moment. "Yeah, it's fair." Deep down she prayed it was a nightmare she would wake up from.

They stood and looked around in silence, a silence that drove Jill crazy. Grabbing the vine, she gave it a good yank. With a firm grip, she took five steps back and grinned. "Dare me?" She kicked off her shoes.

"No." Trevor finally laughed.

"Bet me?" she continued, her laughter ringing through the woods.

"No way." Trevor crossed his arms, standing strong. "I like my money too much."

"Good choice." She wiggled her eyebrows at him as she took off running. Her feet left the path and the trusted old vine from their childhood took her far out to the middle of the lake. Her face lifted to the sky and with eyes wide open, she let go and felt free for the first time in a long time, just like she had when she was a young girl. Within seconds, the cool water washed over her and her feet hit the bottom. She kept herself submerged enjoying the quiet solitude. Then with a hard push, she shot back to the surface. Looking around, she laughed at Trevor who kicked off his shoes grabbing the vine.

"Do a flip!" she shouted with a dare in her voice.

"It's been years since I've even done this," Trevor called back while he backed up the path with the vine. "Let me do it once with just letting go of the damn thing first."

"Chicken," Jill mocked him from the water.

"Smart chicken," he yelled back as he took off running. As his feet left the path and swung out over the water above Jill, he screamed before letting go. "Shiiiiit!"

Jill laughed so hard she could hardly keep herself above water. When he broke the surface, her laughter continued while trying to talk. "Oh, my God, you should have seen your face and you screamed like a girl."

"It's seems a hell of a lot higher than it used to be when we were young and careless." He defended his girly scream with a splash to her face.

She splashed him back and grinned. "Flip?"

He nodded, his grin mirroring hers. "Flip!"

"Whoever screams like a girl buys dinner." Jill laughed, then swallowed a ton of water when he dunked her as he passed.

Jill shouted a threat, swimming hard to catch him, but weakness swallowed her energy forcing her to slow down. Nothing was going to stop her from having this moment with her brother, even if it killed her.

******

Jax pulled into the compound on his bike followed by Blaze and Hunter. His mood was dangerous after his visit with Caroline and by the look of the parking lot, it wasn't going to get much better. Adam paced around throwing his arms all over the place while Slade had his phone to his ear with a grim expression on his face. Instantly, Jax knew this was about Jill.

Stopping in front of Adam, he killed his engine. "She steal your car again?"

"Fuck yeah!" Adam growled, then nodded toward Slade. "I swear if it wasn't for that big son of a bitch, I'd kick her ass."

Jax couldn't help but smirk at that. He knew Adam would never hurt Jill, and Jill would be a tough opponent to take down, even for Adam. "I'm sure she'll be back."

Adam stopped pacing and stared at Jax. "I want my damn car back, now." His pacing started again. "She sucks at driving. I don't want her behind the wheel any longer than she has been already."

"She not answering?" Jax asked Slade, who had joined them.

"No." Fury and concern swirled in Slade's eyes.

"I can find her. I already have her scent." Hunter sat calmly on his bike next to Jax. Reaching into the compartment on his bike, he tossed Blaze a pair of sweats. "Bring these for me."

"Sweet!" Adam said, anxious to get going.

Hunter grabbed the handlebars. "Give me a second to change into my Superman outfit."

Jax actually rolled his eyes. "Where in the fuck did you find that guy?"

Blaze laughed. "He's a pain in the ass, but you'll be thanking me." Smirking, Blaze leaned back on his bike. "He's one hell of a tracker."

Jax hoped to hell so because every day that passes, Mika becomes more dangerous. Within seconds, Hunter the wolf appeared, his gait set with purpose when he stopped where Adam's car had been parked. The wolf's head snapped up and with a confident toss of its head, he took off, expecting everyone to follow.

# CHAPTER 9

Jill watched her brother do a perfect backflip off the vine and sighed. Crap, she was going to have to do better than that or she was going to have to buy dinner. Her and her big mouth. Daring her brother when she felt like shit wasn't the smartest move she had ever made. Yet, she was having a blast. She felt carefree and really needed this moment.

"Eat that!" her brother yelled as he broke surface. "That was definitely a ten."

"Eh, I don't know about a ten, maybe an eight and a half." Jill yelled, her growing grin smug.

"Whatever." Trevor shook his head sending water spraying around him. "Like you could do better. You could never do a backflip without belly flopping."

"So that's my dare." Jill snorted, knowing he was right. She never could do a damn backflip off the vine, but she was part vampire now and was going to make him eat his words while buying her dinner, even if it was a pack of crackers, which seemed to be the only thing that didn't make her nauseous. Feeling weaker by the minute, Jill knew she could pull this last feat off. She didn't have a choice. For once and maybe the last time, she would beat her brother at the backflip contest. Anger and sadness pulsed through her, but she pushed it away.

"Oh, yeah." Trevor huffed as he climbed up the incline toward her. "I can taste that steak and lobster tail bought with your money as we speak. I'm starving."

"You're always starving." Jill snorted.

"And you're stalling." Trevor smirked at her. "Come on with your bad self. Show me what you got."

Jill narrowed her eyes at him and backed up with the vine. Trevor had taken his jeans off and was in his boxers, but Jill kept hers on, stepping on the heavy soggy hems of her pant legs.

Stepping back far enough, her hands tightened, preparing for her final dismount from their trusted vine. With confidence, she glanced at her brother. "Prepare to lose."

Her brother's laughter made her even more determined. Once again, Jill swung over the ledge, letting go at the perfect moment. With everything she had, she put her body into not only one backflip, but two. Seeing the water coming up fast, she hoped she had enough for the second flip. Relief filled her when her feet hit the water first. She'd finally beat her ass of a brother in a backflip contest.

As her feet hit the soft moss-covered bottom, she again used her arms to remain submerged. Looking around the murky bottom, she flinched when a large catfish swam toward her to investigate. How cool was it to be able to stay under as long as she wanted, or at least longer than she had before she was a half-breed. Not wanting to freak her brother out too much, she bent her knees to push off, but a loud muffled noise reached her ears startling her. Before she could turn to see what it was and kick off the bottom, something grabbed her around the waist.

"What in the hell are you doing?" Slade's angry voice boomed as soon as they broke the surface.

"A double backflip." She held onto his shoulders. "Which I killed!" She shouted up at Trevor with triumph. Then it suddenly dawned on her who was holding her and who was surrounding her brother.

On the ledge were Trevor, Adam, Jax, Blaze and a wolf, who she assumed was Hunter, and the damn thing looked like he was grinning, staring down at her. Jill frowned, looking away from the wolf to Slade.

"What are you doing here?" She wiped at the water dripping into her face.

"You stole my car, dammit!" Adam yelled at her.

"Oh, chill out!" Jill yelled back, still looking at a very wet Slade. He did wet really well. "It's in one piece as I'm sure you've already seen, and you weren't going to use it anyway."

"And you knew this because you asked?" Adam stomped toward the ledge, but stopped when loose dirt gave way. "No, you just hotwired it again and rode off without telling anyone. I swear if you mess up my ignition from hotwiring my car, you're going to pay to have it fixed."

Jill snickered. "What is it with him and that piece-of-crap car?"

Slade didn't smile. A frown marred his handsome face.

"You look really sexy wet," Jill whispered, giving him a half grin as she wrapped her legs around him, pressing their wet bodies together. Even though they were both fully clothed, he felt damn good. She never thought she would have Slade in her swimming hole.

"Your lips are turning blue." Slade glared at her lips.

"Then warm them up." Jill went in for the kiss, but his next words stopped her.

"You can't be doing stuff like this, Jill." Slade pulled his head back.

Hoping he wasn't talking about what she thought he was talking about, she frowned. "Okay, I won't hotwire Adam's car anymore." She went back in for the kiss, but he pulled his head further back.

"I don't give a fuck about Adam's car." He growled with a hiss. "You need to take better care of yourself. Keep your strength up until I can fix…."

"Fix me?" Jill tilted her head looking at him. "You can't fix everything, Slade. I'm dying. You said it, everyone sees it and I feel it. I'm not going to lie in a dark room waiting for death."

"I never said you were dying." Slade's eyes shifted for a split second, but it was enough for Jill to see.

"When Hunter said he smelled death, you remained quiet. To me, that's saying more than words ever could." Jill looked toward the empty ledge; everyone had slipped away.

"You are not going to die." Slade grasped her chin, pulling her attention back to him.

Jill stared at him for a long moment before saying anything, as if memorizing his features. "Don't make promises you can't keep, Slade." She kissed his chin, her eyes going back to his. "And don't expect me to wait around doing nothing until that time comes because I can't do that."

He remained silent, but she could see the storm brewing behind his eyes.

"Today with my brother was something that I needed, and now with you here in my childhood swimming hole, it's made this day complete." Jill cupped his cheek. "I'm going to enjoy whatever time I have left instead of living in fear and hope for whatever is to come. It is what it is."

With each word she spoke Slade's eyes turned dark with anger, but she only spoke the truth and he knew it.

"So, now"—she gave him a smile filled with mischief—"I double dog dare you to double back flip off the vine and if you fail, you owe me a full day of being my sex slave." She wiggled her eyebrows at him.

"I'm not finding any of this funny, Jill." Slade's grip tightened on her. He even shook her a little. "You can talk all you want about dying, but I will do whatever it takes to make sure that doesn't happen. First by getting you out of the water."

Deep disappointment ravaged her, tears beat against her eyes, but she held them back. "Then we have a serious problem." She pushed away from him with her weakening strength to swim back to shore, but he grabbed her foot, pulling her back to him.

"No, *you* have a serious problem." Slade's mouth slammed down on hers. He stopped suddenly as he pulled away. "Because even if you end up hating me, you will survive this, as will Pam."

"I could never hate you." Jill once again pushed away. "But I'll never let you change me if it means you will lose everything, and *that* I will fight you about."

A flicker of shock registered before his eyes narrowed. "You need to stop eavesdropping on other people's conversations."

Jill shrugged while she swam backwards. "Seems it's the only way to find out the truth."

"I've never lied to you." Slade swam toward her with predatory ease.

"Keeping information is seen by most as lying." Jill still swimming backwards swam a little faster.

"Seems someone didn't wait around long enough for me to tell her the news." He snatched hold of her feet, pulled her toward him, and wrapped her legs around his waist. "As a matter of fact, she was out breaking the law hotwiring cars."

Jill held on tightly as he walked them out of the water and up the ledge. "Hotwiring that piece of junk isn't breaking the law." Jill rolled her eyes when she heard Adam in the distance still bitching about her taking his car. "But that still doesn't excuse you from lying, Warrior."

Slade didn't set her down once they reached the top, but held her even tighter. "I've told you before I'm a very stubborn male. If I say you will not die, you will not die because no matter what I have to do, fuck the risks, I will do. Nothing will take you from me, Jillian 'soon to be' Buchanan, is that understood?" When she didn't answer, he smacked her wet ass. "I asked you a question."

"Hey!" Jill jerked with a glare.

"Do you understand?" His voice remained hard as he waited for her answer.

"Understood…" Slade always knew when she was lying, so she acted fast to throw him off. "…Master," she added with a sexy twang to her voice.

"I don't believe for a second you meant that." Slade set her on her feet.

"I'll make you a deal." Jill crossed her arms, pushing her wet breasts up, drawing his attention, which of course made her nipples hard as pebbles.

"I don't make deals," he replied without any give in his voice whatsoever, but his eyes skimmed her body.

"Okay, bet." Jill sighed impatiently, but his eyes roaming her wet body was turning her on so badly, her weakness was completely forgotten. His eyes finally met hers with a cocked eyebrow. "If you complete a double backflip off the vine, I will listen to you."

"You will listen to me anyway." Crossing his arms across his massive chest, which was plastered against his wet shirt, he gave her a knowing smirk.

Snapping her eyes off his amazing body, Jill mentally reminded herself with a smack that she didn't take to dominance well unless it was in the bedroom. At present, he was being a dominant ass with no sex promised. She gave him a growl of her own, then laughed. "It's okay. Not many people can pull off a double back flip and I don't want to peer pressure you into anything, but if you pull it off, I'll not only listen to you, I'll be your sex slave."

Slade's head actually fell back as he laughed, but when he snapped his head back, he was more than serious. "You are already my sex slave as I am yours and you will listen to me. Do you understand?"

Jill actually thought she heard herself pant as she nodded. How in the hell could she deny this man anything? Swallowing hard, she leered at him. "Chicken," she whispered, trying her best to ignore his sex slave talk.

Slade's eyes narrowed as he looked out over the water then back to her. "I would do anything for you." With no further words, he took off running, passing the vine, jumping straight up in the air off the ledge and seemed to hover before flipping into not two, but three perfect backflips and, of course, hitting the water in a perfect dive.

"Oh. My. God!" Jill laughed in awe. "That was awesome." She clapped her hands as he swam back and climbed up the ledge.

Shaking the water off his face, he stared down at Jill. "You happy now?"

"Yes!" She laughed then hugged him. "Show me how you did that. I can barely do two and then I belly flop in the water almost every time."

He shook his head taking her arm to lead her away from the water. "No."

"Awe, come on!" she begged with a mischievous grin. "Just once. You said you'd do anything…"

Picking her up in his arms, Slade headed up the path. "You're going to hold that over my head?"

"Absolutely." Jill nodded before resting her head on his chest suddenly tired beyond belief. "Afraid I'll do it better than you?"

Slade's smile didn't reach his eyes. "You know it."

\*\*\*\*\*\*

When Jill didn't answer, Slade looked down at her. She was fast asleep. Hearing the guys up the path, he slowed to a stop to stare at his life in his arms. She *was* his life and the fear of seeing her sick was killing him. He looked composed on the surface—he made damn sure of that—but inside, a fierce desperate panic threatened to consume him.

He had heard talk from other doctors, that they could feel death in their patients, knew when the time was close, and he did also. With Jill, he didn't know if it was his being a doctor, a vampire, or a man in love, but he knew he had to act fast.

A water drop from his wet hair hit her cheek making her flinch, but she didn't wake. Her breathing was even and slow. She had fallen into a deep sleep fast and that worried him. Her pulse beat quickly on the side of her neck, another sign that sent his hidden panic in an uproar. Her coloring was off as well, but that could be due to the cool water. Though he knew that wasn't it. It was just an excuse he could try to use to make it seem like she was okay, when he knew she wasn't.

"What happened?" Trevor's panicked voice broke into his thoughts. "Is she okay?"

Slade nodded, not trusting his voice, but when Trevor's fear for his sister hit him full force, he sighed. "She's just sleeping." Slade walked past Trevor and headed toward Adam's car. He needed to get her out of her wet clothes. Seeing Hunter had shifted back, he nodded toward his bike. "Can you get my bike back to the compound?"

"No problem," Hunter replied, but his eyes stayed on Jill.

"Damn." Adam's face turned from irritation to a worried frown when he opened up the back door of his car. As soon as Slade slid in with Jill still in his arms, Adam closed the door and rushed to jump in.

"Back to the compound?" Adam glanced at Slade in the rearview mirror.

"Yeah and hurry." Slade mumbled a curse when Jill shivered in his arms.

# CHAPTER 10

Jax, Blaze, and Hunter all stood near the bikes watching as Adam backed out of the path with Jill's brother following.

Blaze glanced at Hunter. "You thinking what I'm thinking?"

"If a big juicy steak and red head just as juicy is what you're thinking, then yes." Hunter slid on Slade's bike.

Jax actually grinned at that.

"No, you asshole." Blaze grunted. "Do you think old Mable could help Jill and the others?"

"Crazy-eyed Mable?" Hunter's eyes widened. "Hell, dude, I don't even think she's still alive. The last time I saw her she about made me shit my pants, I'll tell ya."

Blaze laughed. "Garrett told me about that. You ended up having to take Emily Snodgrass to her prom."

"And she told me if I didn't my…and these were her exact words… 'little wiener would shrivel up, turn black and fall off.'" Hunter actually adjusted his crotch. "Let me tell you, boys, when crazy-eyed Mable threatens your dick, you take Emily Snodgrass to the prom."

"Who and what the hell is crazy-eyed Mable?" Jax had never met Hunter, but the guy was funny as hell and actually fit in well with the Warriors, at least with Sid and Jared.

"Some say she's a witch," Hunter replied with a shiver. "But she has this crazy eye that you never know if it's looking at you or not. It just stares off in one direction one minute and the next it's looking straight at you. Creepy as fuck."

"She's not a witch." Blaze frowned, then sighed at Hunter's look. "Okay, she might be a witch. Though she has helped a lot of people."

"Dude, she threatened my dick and called it little. And do you seriously think Dr. Vampire is going to let his mate anywhere close to some crazy old lady with a crazy eye?" Hunter snorted, shaking his head. "Wait, let me answer that for you. Hell no, he's not."

"Just a thought." Blaze glanced at Jax who was grinning. "I seriously never expected Hunter Foster to be afraid of a little old lady."

"Who threatened my dick. Did you not hear that part?" Hunter glared at him.

Jax, still grinning, climbed on the bike. "I just have to ask, why did she make you take this Emily Snodgrass to the prom?"

"Honestly, I was an asshole." Hunter fessed up, actually looking a bit ashamed. "Emily was definitely not my type. She wore these big glasses, was a little on the heavy side, and just not my type. I made fun of Emily one day in town and old Mable heard it. Then she let go with the threats, which as I said scared the shit out of me, so I took Emily to the dance. Funny thing was after the initial embarrassment and after I stopped being a total jerk, Emily was pretty fucking awesome. She was funny and had such a kind heart. She was actually one person I trusted as much as my brothers until she took off to college."

"So you made a great friend—" Jax started, but Hunter interrupted him.

"And saved my dick." Hunter stopped to remind them all of that important information.

"Crazy Mable sounds like a pretty smart woman." Jax nodded to Blaze who nodded back in agreement. "Okay, why don't you guys head down to Tavern's and see if you can find out anything on Mika then I'll meet up with you later."

"Sounds good." Blaze slid on his bike.

"And where are you going?" Hunter grinned with a cocked eyebrow.

Jax's gaze breezed right over Hunter as he started his bike, then kicked it in gear.

"Tell the pretty Caroline I said hello!" Hunter yelled after him, laughing loudly as Jax flipped him off.

\*\*\*\*\*\*

Jax pulled into Caroline's long gravel driveway. It was almost completely dark and he could see what looked like candle light coming from her front window. Parking, he swung off the bike and dug in his bag. Getting what he needed, he headed toward the house, but stopped at the music coming from inside. AC/DC played loudly and Jax grinned. Who knew the proper little school teacher was a heavy metal fan? Closer to the house, he heard her singing along, his grin growing.

Once at the door, he knocked loudly and waited, but the singing continued. Stepping toward the side of the porch, he peered through the window. She stood on a ladder wiping down a wall. His eyes moved down her body. She had changed into a pair of jean shorts, which outlined her heart-shaped ass perfectly. She wasn't a big woman, but she had curves with thighs that could hold a man tight. He was an ass and leg man no doubt, and what he saw, he wanted with a force that shocked him.

Cursing, he backed off to get himself in check. Leaning against the porch railing, he dropped his head back squeezing his eyes shut, but the vision of her on the ladder wouldn't leave.

"Fuck!" he cursed. Wicked visions of her on the ladder, naked, consumed his thoughts. Caught up in the heat, he fell backward, the porch railing breaking against his weight. He tried to land on his feet, but that didn't quite work out because he found himself looking up at the starlit sky. "Son of a bitch!" he cursed again, but this time for a whole different reason and started to stand.

"What do you want?" Caroline's shaky voice and the click of a gun broke the now silent night. AC/DC was no longer playing.

Jax's eyes narrowed as he stared up at Caroline, who was squinting in the darkness, the gun shaking visibly in her hand. "What do I want?" Jax's voice boomed from the darkness. He quickly got up, closing the distance between them, and grabbed the gun before she shot him or herself. "What do I want? Are you kidding me?"

"Jax?" Caroline gasped, then slapped her hand over her heart. "You scared the crap out of me."

"Good." Jax checked the safety on her gun, then stuck it in his pants.

"What was that noise?" Caroline frowned, looking behind him. Her eyes widened. "What happened to my railing?"

Jax glanced back at the rail and then eyed Caroline. Maybe she didn't see his embarrassing fall. "Not sure," he replied, before stepping in front of her to block the broken railing.

Still frowning, she looked up at him. "What are you doing here?"

"I noticed your door locks are old and I wanted to replace them." Jax welcomed the change in topic.

"Oh." Caroline looked at the bag in his hand before looking at him, confused. "Why?"

"Because you shouldn't be staying here alone without good locks on your doors," Jax replied, irritated. "That's why. And if you ever have to point a gun at a man again, you better have a steady hand and do not, under any circumstance, ask him what he wants."

Caroline bit her lip, folding her arms. "Well, I wasn't expecting anyone—"

"Always expect someone." Jax frowned down at her. "If you plan on staying here alone, you need to expect and be ready for some asshole to come sniffing around."

She rolled her eyes, her frown deepening. "No one is going to come sniffing around." She held out her hand. "Can I have my gun back, please?"

Jax ignored her and headed over to a small kitchen table, which was the only furniture in the place. Glancing down at a plate, he picked it up, looking at it closely. "What the hell is this?"

Caroline walked over, snatching the plate from his hand. "Dinner." She put the plate back on the table.

The burned-to-a-crisp hamburger was eaten on the edges only and the lonely hotdog was so black and deformed he felt sorry for it. "That's food?" He couldn't help but ask with a snort.

"Yeah, smartass." Caroline slammed her hand on her hip. "I had a little trouble with the grill, but it was perfect." The disgusted crinkle of her nose revealed her lie.

Cocking his eyebrow at the food, Jax pulled out his phone and shot off a text. "You have any tools?"

"You really don't have to do this," Caroline said, her face blushing beautifully.

Jax stared at her without saying a word, waiting for her answer.

With a huff, Caroline went to the corner, bent over to grab a tiny toolbox, making Jax groan, and then set it on the table with a glare. "Anything else?" Her tone was definitely not pleasant.

Now wasn't that a loaded question. Jax watched her, appreciating how beautiful she looked in candlelight. Staying clear of her was sure going to hell, he cursed to himself. She had a vulnerability to her that drew him in, plus she was beautiful, smart and what the fuck was wrong with him? Next he'd be kneeling at her fucking feet spouting poetry. "Fuck!" He growled, grabbing the tiny toolbox and heading toward the front door.

Before long, he had fixed both locks and had tried them multiple times before handing her the keys.

"Thank you." Caroline took the keys.

"You're welcome." Jax rolled his shoulders, becoming

uncomfortable and was glad to hear the motorcycles coming up the road. "Make sure you have these doors locked, both of them."

"Why are you doing this when you so adamantly stated you wanted nothing to do with me?" Caroline looked up from the keys in her hand, true confusion coloring her voice and shadowing her eyes.

Caroline's question was fair and Jax knew it. He just didn't know how to answer her. And he never said he wanted nothing to do with her. He had warned her to stay away from him, which to be fair, she had. He was the one having a hard time, and wasn't that a kick in the balls. The knock on the door saved him from saying anything at all.

"Who in the world can that be?" The knock startled Caroline.

Jax knew she hadn't heard the bikes because of the music playing, something else that bothered him. Anyone could sneak up without her even knowing it. He watched her walk to the door and followed her. She was about to open the door without asking who it was, but he slammed his hand against it, preventing her.

"Never open the door without knowing who's on the other side, Caroline." Jax dropped his gaze to hers, her scent enveloping him in warmth. "Wouldn't you tell your kids the same thing?"

Caroline's glare softened with understanding. "Who is it?" she asked loudly, but her eyes stayed on Jax. He could have sworn she inhaled his scent as well.

"Pizza and my friend, beer. Now open the door. Pizza is getting cold and beer is getting warm, plus you have the biggest fucking mosquitoes out here that I ever saw. Blaze is fighting one as I speak." Hunter's voice came through the door. "Shoot the bastard."

Jax grinned as he removed his hand from the door. Even though he knew exactly who had been out there, he wanted Caroline to realize living on her own in the middle of nowhere was dangerous. She needed to be smart and safe.

Laughing, Caroline opened the door wide letting them in. Blaze was actually swatting at something buzzing around his head. "I didn't order pizza," she said as Hunter passed her with three boxes. Blaze passed also, carrying a case of beer.

"He did." Hunter nodded toward Jax and headed to the table.

"I didn't order beer." Jax caught one that Blaze tossed him.

"That was all me." Hunter grinned, catching a beer in one hand while setting the pizzas on the table.

"What about me?" Caroline frowned, staring at Blaze who was setting the beer on the floor. Blaze gave her an approving nod, grabbing one out of the box and handing it to her. "Thank you." She smiled.

"What in the holy hell is that?" Hunter picked up the paper plate bringing it to his face. "Is that a hot dog?"

"I had a little trouble with the grill." Blushing, Caroline grabbed the plate and tossed it in the garbage bag.

"I'd say." Hunter snorted, shaking his head. Opening one of the pizza boxes, he pushed it toward her.

"Kind of looked like what old crazy-eyed Mable was going to do with yours." Blaze chuckled and leaned against the wall.

"Not funny." Hunter glared at the garbage, then to Blaze. "But an uncanny resemblance."

When Caroline frowned at Jax, he just shook his head with a chuckle. "Don't ask."

# CHAPTER 11

Slade hung up the phone as Pam and Duncan walked in his office with Sloan close on their heels. Seeing Pam, he frowned. She was extremely pale, her cheeks sunk in. She was deteriorating fast which made him wonder exactly how long she had been sick.

"I'm sorry Duncan hasn't been at work much." Pam looked up at Sloan.

"Damon, Jared, Sid, and Jax have things under control." Sloan offered her a smile. "You just worry about getting yourself better."

Sloan's eyes widened when Pam reached out, hugging him before quickly letting go. "Thank you."

"Any news?" Duncan's voice was harsh with worry as he helped Pam up on the examining table to sit.

Sloan cleared his throat, his gaze still on Pam. "Not yet." He finally shifted his attention to Duncan and Slade. "I'm trying to set up a hearing ASAP, but so far nothing."

Duncan cursed and took hold of Pam's hand. He spoke to Slade. "What about you?"

"I just got off the phone with an old colleague of mine from California." Slade actually felt some hope, and it must have shown on his face because Pam sat up straighter, her eyes clearing.

"Do they know what to do to help us that won't get you guys arrested?" Her voice sounded as weak as she looked.

"They've been injecting vampire blood into the half-breeds who are under their care, like a blood transfusion. They seem to be tolerating it more intravenously than actually feeding." Slade began, but held up his hand when they all three started to talk at once. "It's dangerous and it may not work. It has worked with some, but not others, and on some it makes them sicker. For the ones who it has helped, they don't know how long the results will last."

"Do it." Pam's voice strengthened with hope.

Slade frowned. "Pam, there are risks and you really need to think about this before we jump in—"

"I'm getting weaker by the day." Pam's voice shook. "I can't even pick up Daniel anymore. If there is a possibility that this will work to buy us time, then I want it done now."

Glancing at Duncan waiting for his approval, Pam grabbed Slade's arm, drawing his attention back to her.

"This is my decision," Pam added before looking up at Duncan. "It's my risk to take."

Duncan's face was void of emotion, but his eyes expressed his turmoil. "What do we need to do?"

"Pam, why don't you go be with Daniel for a little while." Slade's phone beeped behind him. "I need to take some blood from Duncan and then we'll start."

Nodding, Pam let Duncan help her off the table. "Have you done this with Jill yet?" she asked before leaving.

"No, not yet," Slade replied, glancing at his phone.

Pam nodded with one last glance at Duncan before walking out the door and leaving the three Warriors alone.

"So are you using Pam as a trial before giving it to Jill?" Duncan's mood turned dangerous as soon as Pam was out of hearing range.

Sloan took a step forward, but didn't comment.

Slade looked up from his phone, his expression furious. "I'm going to ignore that, you son of a bitch because I know how worried you are." Slade slammed his phone down. "Jill has a fever and is not a good candidate for this, yet. I will check Pam over before I attempt to even try this, so keep your fucking attitude to yourself and know I am trying to save not only your mate, but mine as well."

Duncan stepped back and sighed. "Sorry, man, I'm just—"

"I know." Slade took a deep breath trying to calm himself down. If he were in Duncan's shoes, he probably would have thought the same thing.

"Is Jill okay?" Sloan asked, giving Duncan a moment to regain his composure.

"Nicole and Tessa are with her now in our room." Slade cleared his throat. "She stole Adam's car to go see her brother."

"Again?" Sloan shook his head, a small grin slipping across his lips.

"Yeah." Slade also grinned. "Hunter tracked her down and we found her and her brother jumping from a vine into a lake. She was having the time of her life, but I think it was too much for her weakening system because now she's running a fever." His smile slipped away as quickly as it appeared.

No one said a word. Three of the most feared Warriors stood in Slade's office staring into space, at a total loss of what to do. Anything that threatened their own, they could deal with and had dealt with, but this was something different. It seemed as though all the odds were stacked against them.

"I won't let them die," Slade repeated. He hoped that if he said it enough, it would be the truth.

"Promise me one thing." Duncan looked up from the floor. "Tell me when it's time, because I will not let Pam die when changing her could save her life. She refused to let me change her now because of her fear for me, but—"

"I will let you know, brother," Slade promised, placing his large hand on Duncan's shoulder.

Duncan looked at Sloan. "If anything happens to me, I want your promise to take care of my family."

"If I'm not rotting in the jail cell with you, you have my promise," Sloan vowed.

"No, you need to stay neutral," Duncan replied. "You're the only thing that keeps us going. Without your leadership, everything we've achieved will be lost."

Slade nodded in agreement. "He's right." Slade scrubbed Duncan's arm, prepping him to take his blood for Pam. "We're going to need someone in our corner on the outside who has the contacts you do. This is going to get worse before it gets better."

Sloan cursed. "Has Adam showed any signs?"

Looking up from Duncan's arm, Slade frowned. "Not yet, but it's only a matter of time. It's seems no manmade half breed is immune."

\*\*\*\*\*\*

Caroline sat in the middle of the floor in her new home eating pizza and drinking beer with three of the most handsome men she had ever laid eyes on. Wouldn't the parents of her students be gossiping up a storm if they saw her now? The prim and proper Ms. Fitzpatrick gone wild.

"So are you two VC Warriors?" Caroline asked Blaze and Hunter who were finishing off the last box of pizza.

"Hell no." Hunter snorted. "I'm a shifter, not vampire, and I guess the VC Warriors are too good for shifters."

"A shifter?" Caroline finished off her second beer and decided it probably should be her last. She wasn't a big drinker and she was starting to feel it. "You mean you can shift into a rabbit or something?"

Blaze choked on his pizza while Jax chuckled.

"Excuse me?" Hunter stared at her. "Did you say a...rabbit?"

Caroline smiled. "Well, yes, but I mean, can't shifters shift into anything they want to shift into?" Taking in the look of horror on his face, she realized she'd offended him. "I mean, I think you'd make a cute rabbit."

"Oh, shit." Blaze tossed the rest of his uneaten pizza in the box. "That is the funniest damn thing I've ever heard."

Hunter ignored him. "I would make a badass rabbit, but no." He sat up straighter. "I belong to the Lee County Wolf Pack. I am a wolf shifter and my wolf is not very happy with you at the moment. A rabbit…are you kidding me? Who the fuck would want to shift into a rabbit?"

"Sorry." Caroline tried to sound sincere, but the giggle ruined it. "And what about you?" she asked Blaze who was still laughing at Hunter.

"I'm like him." He nodded toward Jax. "Vampire slash shifter."

"So you're a VC Warrior." Caroline noticed a mood shift.

"No," Blaze replied without any explanation.

Caroline glanced at Jax, who just cocked an eyebrow at her as if saying 'you're on your own.' Her attention went back to Hunter. "Can you show me your wolf?"

"I love when women ask me that." Hunter winked at her before wiggling his eyebrows.

"Hunter," Jax warned with a shake of his head.

Rolling his eyes, Hunter looked at Caroline. "I would, but I don't want to ruin these clothes and I didn't bring any others with me. Unless you want to see me naked, then we can work something—" Jax threw an empty beer can at Hunter shutting him up.

Caroline's face heated. "I'll pass, but thanks for the warning."

"Your loss." Hunter winked at her again then acted like he was ready to bat away another beer can, but the only thing Jax threw Hunter's way was a warning glare.

She looked at Blaze. "How about you? Can you shift into something, now? Fully clothed of course," she added quickly.

Blaze seemed more relaxed with that question, and in the blink of an eye, he transformed into Hunter. Stunned, Caroline's mouth gaped open.

"Hi. My name is Hunter," Blaze said, mimicking Hunter's voice with precision. "I like shifting into cute furry rabbits."

"Oh, ha-ha." Hunter rolled his eyes. "Real funny, asshole."

Caroline laughed. "That's amazing." She watched as Blaze's eyes started swirling as he turned to look toward Hunter, who was still griping about Blaze being an asshole. In awe, she looked on as Hunter's boot started to smoke. A tiny flame sparked out from the tip and the real Hunter jumped up.

"Dammit, Blaze!" Hunter danced around trying to put out the flame. "These are my favorite boots."

"Guess I don't have to ask how you got your name." She looked toward Blaze who was himself once again.

Blaze nodded. "For a human you seem to take all this pretty well, especially since shifters haven't come out like the vampires."

"That's because we're smarter than vampires." Hunter finally sat back down, his boot no longer on fire.

"Well, my sister's mated to Sid and..." She shifted uncomfortably looking over Hunter's head. "...I talk to dead people."

"You talk to what?" Hunter tilted his head toward her with a frown.

"Dead people," she replied once again, looking past Hunter. "So it takes a lot to freak me out."

"Why do you keep looking over my head?" Hunter frowned, then laughed with a snort. "Good one, pretty lady. For a minute there, you had me going."

"She can talk to dead people." Jax grinned, enjoying Hunter's discomfort.

"So can my sister." Caroline smirked. "We're twins and have the same gift."

Blaze and Hunter openly stared at her, probably like she had been staring at them a few minutes ago. "What?"

"How many dead people do you see and is there one behind me?" Hunter's eyes narrowed at her.

Caroline looked behind Hunter and shook her head. "He moved."

"Where?" Hunter was now downright glaring at her.

"He's sitting next to you." Caroline backed away as Hunter shot up to his feet, tripping toward Jax.

"He's just a child." Caroline smiled at the empty space, but her head moved as if watching an invisible person walking toward Hunter. "And he likes you. You make him laugh."

That took Hunter back. "Who is he?"

"Not sure." Caroline glanced at Jax, who was staring at her with an odd look on his face. "He was here when I purchased the house."

"And you still bought this place? Woman, you're crazy!" Hunter yelled, looking at her like she'd lost her mind.

"You scared him." Caroline frowned.

"Yeah, well….sorry!" Hunter yelled out to the air. "But honestly, the only dead thing I ever deal with are vampires, but I can see those suckers. No offense."

"None taken," Jax said smirking, enjoying watching Hunter squirm.

Caroline watched Blaze closely and could tell he was uncomfortable, and he should be. He had at least ten dead people following him around. She had seen them the first time she met him, but kept her mouth shut because, well, it could be a little unsettling for people. Taking in his attitude, she figured she'd continue to stay quiet...for now.

Jax's phone rang, breaking the uncomfortable silence. "Yeah," Jax answered, his eyes going to Hunter, then to Blaze. "Be there in ten."

Jax stood along with Blaze. Caroline started to stand on her own, but three huge hands appeared in front of her face. Grabbing one without looking at who it belonged to, she was eased to her feet. She stared into Jax's golden stare. "Thank you."

"You're welcome," he replied, letting go of her hand quickly. "We need to go. Let's get this cleaned up."

"That's okay. You guys go ahead." Caroline took an empty pizza box out of Blaze's hand. "Is everything okay?"

Before Jax could answer, Hunter became instantly alert. "Do dead people carry a scent?"

Caroline just stared at him as if he were being a smartass.

"Do dead people carry a scent?" he asked again, his voice sharp. He went from funny guy to deadly in a second flat.

"No, not really," Caroline replied, looking confused as Jax took a protective step closer to her.

"Someone who doesn't belong here is very close." Hunter sniffed the air.

"Go!" Jax pulled Caroline out of the way.

Hunter began to shake, his body contorting in front of her very eyes and Caroline actually grabbed ahold of Jax. Within seconds, a huge beautiful wolf stood before her and she wondered briefly if she had more beers than she thought. With a loud growl, he turned his head to look straight at her and then to Jax as if waiting for orders.

"Track and see what you can find." Jax nodded toward Blaze who went to open the door. "We'll meet you back at the compound."

Caroline watched this wild animal take orders from Jax and knew it was Hunter, but still it was almost too much for her mind to take. Then the wolf looked at her once more.

"Don't worry, she's going with us," Jax answered the unspoken question.

"What?" Caroline said surprised, but couldn't take her eyes off the wolf until it was out of sight. Then she looked up at Jax. "I've got work to do. I can't leave and plus I have a gun."

"No, *I've* got your gun." Jax left her and locked the back door as Blaze blew out the candle, leaving Caroline no choice but to go with them. "I'll bring you back after Hunter makes sure it's safe."

Caroline dug her heels in. "I'm not going anywhere."

Jax sighed, tightening his grip on her arm. "You are going, so you better grab whatever you need on the way out." He narrowed his eyes as he leaned in close. "I warned you to stay away from me."

"You're the one who came to me," she shot back, leaning even closer, her eyes just as narrow

"So I did, didn't I?" Jax's lips were so close to hers she could feel his breath, but then he was gone and she was being pulled behind him wondering what in the hell he meant with those words.

# CHAPTER 12

Jill could feel someone staring at her before she even opened her eyes and opening her eyes was not an easy feat. It felt like they were sewed shut. She could hear whispering, but couldn't make out any of the words. It was definitely female voices. Oh, God, was it her wedding day and she passed out? Fighting to wake up, her eyes slowly opened.

"Did I mess up the dress?" Jill croaked. Her dry throat made it difficult to swallow.

Tessa's face came into view. "What dress?" Tessa asked, touching Jill's forehead. "How are you feeling?"

"My wedding dress." Jill tried to swallow again. "Did I tear it?"

"She must still have a fever." Nicole also leaned over her.

"No, she feels cool to me." Tessa removed her hand. "You feel her."

Jill brushed Nicole's hand off trying to sit up. "I need water." Again she tried to swallow, but it was nearly impossible. Finally looking around, she realized it wasn't her wedding and she was in her and Slade's bed.

Tessa ran to the bathroom then came back quickly with a glass of water. Jill tried not to down it in one swallow, but it felt so good sliding down her throat.

"Slow down," Nicole scolded, sitting on the bed next to her.

Too late. Her stomach cramped painfully. Handing the glass back to Tessa, she lay back rubbing her stomach.

"Listen, Jill, we're sorry." Tessa came out of the bathroom and sat down on the other side of her. "We've been bugging the hell out of you about this wedding. We didn't know you were sick."

"No, we didn't," Nicole grumbled. "And Damon got hell for not telling me."

Jill grinned even though it was the last thing she felt like doing. "I bet he did, but honestly, I wasn't even sure what was going on."

"Damon and Jared finally told us everything." Nicole put her hand on Jill's. "Don't worry. Slade will find out what's going on and will help you and Pam."

"Where is Slade?" Jill opened one eye to look at Nicole then Tessa.

"He's with Pam." Tessa glanced at Nicole, then back to Jill. "He wanted us to stay with you until he gets back."

"Why's he with Pam?" Jill sat back up, her chest tight with fear. "Is she okay?"

"I'm sure she's fine," Nicole replied. "Just lie back and rest for a while."

An inhuman roar filled the room making each woman jump and stared at the door.

"What in the hell was that?" Tessa clutched her chest, eyes fixed on the door as if whatever made that God awful noise was going to come into the room at any minute.

Running feet passed, heading down the hallway. Jill jumped out of bed, grabbed a pair of shorts and she swung open the door, following Sid and Jared who were running toward Slade's office. She managed to get her feet in her shorts as she ran. Before turning the corner, she heard the commotion of shouts, grunts and all out hell fire coming from Slade's office.

With no thought at all, she ran to the open doorway, her eyes landing on a horror she would never be able to forget. Jared grabbed a screaming Tessa, taking her out of the room. Nicole pushed past Jill, but all Jill could do was stare in shock.

"Get her the fuck out of here!" Slade bellowed.

Jill's eyes swung to his as someone grabbed her around the waist taking her out of the room. Her last vision was Slade covered in blood, Pam laying lifeless on the examination table, and Duncan being restrained by Sid and Sloan.

"No!" Jill screamed, fighting to get to Pam. "No!"

\*\*\*\*\*\*

Jax opened the door for Caroline and followed her into the compound. Lana was just coming down the steps.

"Hey, there you are." Lana hugged Caroline. "I got your message. What's going on?"

"Hunter picked up someone's scent around her place so he's checking it out. I thought it was best that she come back with me and Blaze until we got the all clear from Hunter." Jax headed toward Sloan's office. "Where is everyone? Sloan wanted us here."

"Not sure. They'll probably be back. Sid left a little bit ago for the meeting. They should be in Sloan's office or maybe the game room?" Lana frowned. "I was upstairs with Katrina playing with Daniel."

"You hear anything from Hunter?" Jax asked Blaze as he leaned against the doorjamb to Sloan's office.

"No, not yet." Blaze checked his phone before answering.

"So what do you think of my sister's new place?" Lana grinned at Jax.

"Yeah, about that." Caroline glared at Lana. "Are you in the habit of giving out my address to anyone?"

"I didn't give it to anyone." Lana shot back with a knowing grin. "I gave it to Jax. It's a dump, isn't it?" she said to Jax, ignoring Caroline's glare.

"You've just been officially uninvited to my first dinner party," Caroline snapped.

"How about uninviting me to help you paint?" Lana grinned. "That would really devastate me."

Jax opened his mouth to say something, but a roar of rage took them all by surprise. Blaze was the first to take off toward the noise with Jax close on his heels. "Get in Sloan's office and lock yourselves in," he shouted to Lana and Caroline as he disappeared.

"Hell with that." Lana grabbed Caroline as she ran after Jax and Blaze. "Stay behind me."

Caroline kept up with Lana who was in much better shape, but the closer they got, the more she wished they would have listened to Jax and locked themselves in Sloan's office. It was total chaos. Jared was rushing past with Tessa, who was crying uncontrollably. Screams and shouts were coming out of a room right before them. Jax and Blaze disappeared into the room, but Blaze returned, carrying a kicking and screaming Jill away.

Her mind screamed for her to stop, but her feet kept following Lana until the door slammed, shutting them out.

Blaze had finally gotten Jill calmed down and Jared was coming back with Tessa held close to his side. Steve, Adam, and Angelina followed.

"What happened?" Lana's voice shook as she looked at Jared. "Please tell me it's not Sid."

Jared grabbed her with his free arm, holding her close. "No, it's not Sid." Jared stared at the door. "Slade was giving Pam a blood transfusion using Duncan's blood."

Jill pulled away from Blaze. "Why was he doing that?" Jill looked up at Jared. "Did she get worse?"

"Honey, I don't know." Jared frowned down at her. "Something went wrong and—"

"And what?" Jill's voice filled with panic.

"And Slade is going to take care of her." Steve walked over, wrapping his arm around Jill and answering for Jared who for once seemed to be at a loss for words.

Caroline and Lana shared a look as the door opened. Duncan walked out, his face ravaged with pain and despair as he carried Pam's lifeless body in his arms. They were both covered in blood. He stared straight ahead, daring anyone to stop him. Nicole followed close behind him, her face streaked with tears. She stopped in front of Caroline. "He wants you and Lana."

Putting her hand to her mouth, Caroline nodded as her eyes filled up with tears. She jerked when someone touched her arm.

"I told you to go in Sloan's office." Jax's voice was low and deep.

Again Caroline nodded, which was all she could do, afraid if she opened her mouth, a scream of horror would escape. As she looked up at Jax, her tears escaped, rolling down her cheeks in waves. Jax cursed, taking her into his arms, holding her tightly.

******

Jill's body quaked from heartbreak as she watched Duncan carrying Pam. She stumbled out of his way as he passed, his eyes straight ahead not once flicking toward her or anyone for that matter. She watched until he disappeared and then hurried toward Slade's office. Not paying attention, she slipped on the blood-soaked floor, but Blaze, who had followed her, caught her before she hit the ground.

"Don't turn him in until we know…" Sid stopped talking as soon as he spotted her.

"Turn him in?" Jill frowned, her eyes searching for answers to what was going on. The examination table, the floor, the walls, Sloan, Sid, and Slade were all splattered with blood.

"Jill, you shouldn't be here," Slade replied, not looking at her. "Take her out," he ordered Blaze, but Jill jerked her arm away.

"You can't turn him in. Duncan turned her, didn't he?" Jill wasn't leaving until she was ready. No one said a word. No one would look at her. She walked straight up to Sloan. "You can't turn him in."

"He doesn't have a choice." Sid's voice rose, truly indicating how upset he really was.

"Yes, he does." Jill's voice rose right back. "Don't turn him in. It's as easy as that."

"You know nothing." Sid growled as he walked past her and out the door.

Jill ignored Sid as he brushed past, but continued to stare at Sloan, who had finally looked at her. "Daniel needs him," she pleaded. "No one has to know what happened. No one here will say anything, you know that."

Sloan didn't say anything. He walked past her and out the door, slamming it hard behind him. Jill turned to see Slade, his eyes vacant, as he stared at her.

"What happened?" She couldn't decide if she should walk up to him or not. He seemed unapproachable and that scared her. Hell, everything at this point scared her and she didn't like it. When he didn't answer, she edged closer to him. "Slade?" she whispered.

His whispered name seemed to pull him out of wherever his mind had gone. With no warning whatsoever, he pulled her to him, holding her tightly. "I screwed up." He held her tighter, almost breaking her in half. His voice was ragged with emotion. "I shouldn't have…"

Not really knowing what happened, Jill didn't know what to say. Pulling back to look up into his eyes, she saw defeat. That was the kicker. Any defeat in this man's eyes was their downfall and it couldn't happen.

"Look at me." Jill grabbed his face, forcing his eyes to hers. "I love you."

His eyes hardening at her words wasn't the effect she was going for.

"I don't know what happened here, but I know you tried your best." Jill wouldn't let him look away. "You can't give up, Slade. I need you."

She knew she was putting more pressure on him, but she didn't know what else to say, what else to do. The glazed look in his eyes cleared and she knew it was working.

"I need you," Jill repeated, placing a kiss on his firm lips. "I will always need you, but now more than ever."

Slade's eyes left hers, scanning his blood-covered office. "I warned them. I told them the risks." His eyes came back to hers. "But in the end, it was me they were looking to for guidance. I was told the transfusions worked for some for a short period, but not others. She wasn't strong enough and her body went into shock. Fuck! I should have known she was too weak."

"But he changed her." Jill fought for him. "That is what would have had to happen eventually, right?"

"It may have been too late. I promised my brother I would let him know when it was time and I failed. He may have been too late." Slade cursed again, walking away from her. "I need to go check on her."

She watched as he collected a few items, throwing them in a bag. He stopped at the door turning his head, but he didn't look at her over his shoulder. "I love you."

Before Jill could respond, he rushed out the door. Tears flowed down her cheeks. She wasn't afraid for herself; she was afraid for him. If Pam didn't make it, losing her would ruin Slade. Wiping her face, she looked around the office and knew what needed to be done. He didn't need to come back to his office and see this as a reminder of what happened.

Grabbing as many towels as she could, Jill tossed them on Slade's desk, except for one. Turning, she stared at the examination table as more tears threatened to fall. As she stared at the blood, Jill knew she would never forget the sound of pure anguish that had rose from Duncan's throat. That had to be what hell sounded like. Squeezing her eyes shut, she put her hands over her ears trying to block out the memory.

Feeling someone take the towel from her hand, she opened her eyes to find Adam looking down at her. Turning, he walked away and began cleaning up Slade's office. Steve and Angelina worked side by side doing the same. Taking a deep breath, Jill once again wiped her tears away, grabbed another towel and went to work. A Warrior never gave up. They may get knocked down, but they never stayed down, and she *was* a Warrior.

# CHAPTER 13

Caroline slowly opened her eyes, a streak of bright sunlight blinding her momentarily. Tilting her head, she looked around the room from her position in a chair she had propped herself in to get a few hours of sleep. She hadn't stepped foot out of Duncan and Pam's small apartment for three days, neither had Nicole or Lana. They ate, showered and slept while waiting for Pam to pull through, praying for her survival.

Moving only her eyes, she saw Pam laying in the bed in the same position, with Duncan holding her hand, staring down at her with such hope, love and despair that it actually hurt her heart to keep looking at them. Shifting her eyes away from them, they landed on Jax who was staring directly at her from across the room where he leaned against the wall, arms crossed. In these three days, she had learned more about Jax Wheeler than she ever would have, even though they had hardly spoken. His devotion to his fellow Warrior was beyond belief, and his care for her, Nicole, and Lana was just as impressive.

She couldn't stop staring at him. It was as if her soul sought him out and couldn't let go once it found him. Neither she nor Lana had been left alone in the room without one Warrior with them, and she knew why, without anyone telling her. If Pam didn't pull out of this, Duncan would be out of control with sorrow and rage. It was for their protection as well as Duncan's. If Jax was gone, another Warrior took his place. Even Sloan had kept vigil. Slade was in and out, his duty split between Pam and Jill. His focus and determination were admirable, but she saw in Slade's eyes that Pam's future was out of his hands now.

Finally closing her eyes, she rubbed her face, and then sat up slowly. In her younger days, this chair would have been no problem, but it was kicking her ass. She stretched, trying to work out the stiffness. A moment later, Nicole brought her a cup of coffee. Taking it, she smiled a thanks, her eyes searching for Lana. She found her in Sid's arms on the floor. Sid looked up from watching Lana, giving her a wink.

At first, she had been confused why Duncan would want her with him during this time of such personal sadness, but then she realized why before it was explained to her by Nicole. He wanted her and Lana there just in case Pam didn't make it. She wasn't sure of the exact reason, but knew it had to do with their gifts and honestly, she didn't care what it was. She was there to help in any way she could.

She, Nicole, and Lana had wanted to help clean the blood from Pam that night, but Duncan had refused with an aggressiveness that honestly scared Caroline, but she understood it. So she had kept her distance and watched as this strong Warrior had heartbreakingly taken care of his mate.

Caroline shivered with anxious aggravation. For two of the three days in this room, something had been nagging at her and it was starting to drive her crazy. With her coffee that had been her lifeline, she quietly walked over to Sid and Lana. Kneeling on the ground, she gently nudged her sister. Sid frowned at her for waking up Lana, but Caroline just frowned back at him.

"What?" Lana grumbled, then sat up quickly, looking over at the bed in panic.

"Do you feel it?" Caroline whispered low enough she was sure Duncan couldn't hear her.

Lana sat up surprisingly focused for just waking up. The sisters stared at each other for a long minute. "Yeah, I do." Lana frowned. "Who is it?"

"I don't know, but I think whoever it is, they're right." Caroline downed the rest of her coffee.

"Is it Pam?" The worried tone in Sid's voice rang true. His body became suddenly tense as his eyes shot to Duncan.

"No," both Lana and Caroline reassured him.

Relief shadowed his features, but then he frowned. "Then who are you talking about?"

Jax had walked over and was standing over them. "She needs something to fight for." Caroline looked at Nicole who also joined them.

"And that something has been sitting at her side without moving an inch for three days," Sid replied, his frown deepening.

"A woman would walk through hellfire for their man, but a mother would fight the devil himself for her child." Caroline looked back over at Pam and knew she was right, or at least knew whoever put that thought in her head was right.

"Duncan won't allow it." Sid shook his head.

The three women looked at each other with determination. "I'll get Daniel." Nicole stood, but stopped when Sid grabbed her leg. "Let go, Sid."

"Did you hear me?" Sid hissed. "Duncan will not allow this. You're going to upset him and he doesn't need this shit right now."

Nicole jerked her leg away. "This isn't about Duncan," she hissed back. "And I'm not going to lose my best friend because it might upset Duncan."

"Shit." Sid stood, glancing at Duncan who seemed to be oblivious to anything other than Pam. "I'll go get Damon and Slade." He quietly left the room.

"So you really think this will work?" Jax also glanced at Pam.

"For some weird reason, yes," Lana said. "It happens this way sometimes. We get messages or thoughts without having any clue where they come from or who it comes from, but we've learned to listen."

"How long does it usually take for someone to..." Caroline frowned trying to find the right words. "...change?" This vampire thing was new to her.

"It really depends." Jax stared down at her. "The problem is Pam was weak before the change."

The door opened and in walked Nicole holding Daniel, followed by Slade, Damon, and Sid. Caroline walked closer, amazed at how much Daniel looked like Pam. His curious eyes looked around the room at everyone, a huge smile on his face. What mother wouldn't fight to come back to this adorable child?

Daniel turned his head, his bright blue eyes landing on Pam. "Mommy." His little voice broke the silence, his outstretched arms reaching for Pam.

Duncan's head swiveled from Pam to his son. His eyes growing dangerously dark as he gently released Pam's hand and stood. "What are you doing?" His eyes pinned Nicole to the spot. When he took a step forward, Damon also moved ready to protect Nicole.

Feeling that this was her plan, Caroline also stepped forward. "It was my idea." Caroline cleared her throat nervously when Duncan's eyes blazed toward her.

"You had no right." Duncan's eyes swung around as he ignored Daniel's pitiful plea to go to him. "None of you had any right to make this decision."

She felt Jax at her back and swallowed hard. It was do or die time. Her eyes flickered to Pam then to Duncan. Now more than ever, death was close. No one needed her gift to feel that.

"If Pam has a fighting chance to come through this, she needs something to fight for." Caroline made damn sure her voice was strong with conviction, because Duncan looked like he wanted to kill her. "If Daniel were my son, I would do everything in my power to get back to him. Any mother would and if you would look past your own pain, you would see this is what needs to be done."

The room was deathly silent. Caroline went to Nicole reaching out toward Daniel who looked away from Pam and reached for her. Smiling at the young boy, she stopped directly in front of Duncan who continued to stare at her.

"Daddy," Daniel said, his tone more reserved as he looked at Duncan. As if knowing something wasn't right, his little arms wrapped around her neck tighter.

Seeing something flicker in Duncan's eyes, she held Daniel out to him. "Make her fight."

Duncan finally looked away from her to Daniel, then took him in his arms. Father and son stared at each other before Daniel reached up, lightly patting Duncan on the cheek and that was when Duncan broke. He turned away from everyone holding Daniel close to his chest.

Caroline watched Daniel's little arms reach up to wrap around Duncan's neck and she lost it. Putting her hand over her mouth, she turned, running right into Jax, who once again, wrapped her in his arms.

Daniel's little face peeked around Duncan's shoulder to look at Pam. Then he reached for her. Duncan turned, then sat, scooting the chair closer to Pam and sitting Daniel on the bed.

Taking one finger, Daniel poked Pam in the arm, and then pulled his hand away holding it close to his body before looking up at Duncan, then back to Pam. Surprisingly careful for a three-year-old, Daniel inched his way up the bed and lightly patted Pam's cheek. He frowned when Pam didn't respond. "Sleepy?" His little voice broke every heart in the room.

Duncan cleared his throat and nodded. "Yes, Mommy's sleeping."

Daniel looked away from Duncan before resting his head on her chest. With his little hand, he patted her softly.

Enemies far and wide looked for a way to bring the VC Warriors to their knees, that much Caroline knew. Wouldn't they be shocked that all it took was a little freckle-faced boy's love for his mother?

\*\*\*\*\*\*

Jill lay on her back in the middle of the floor in Pam and Duncan's apartment playing airplane rides with Daniel. It had been five days since Duncan had tried to change Pam, two of those days with Daniel being brought in to be with Pam and Duncan. Everyone took turns keeping the active toddler entertained.

Slade walked in and stood over them. He chuckled when Daniel tried to make airplane noises. "How you feeling?" He leaned down, feeling her forehead.

"I'm fine." Jill grinned at Daniel who was slobbering all over the place while making airplane sounds. "But I may drown in drool."

Daniel laughed when Jill started to make the noises along with him.

"Don't wear yourself out," Slade ordered, his eyes intense as he stared down at her.

"Any improvement?" Jill brushed past Slade's order.

Slade glanced toward Pam with a confident stare. "Yes, she's starting to heal herself. The bruising from the needles is gone as are the wounds from being changed." Slade didn't say much with Daniel there. "It's a great sign."

Relief filled Jill. The past five days have been hell and everything had stopped, except for their vigil over Pam. "I knew you could pull her through."

"It had nothing to do with me," Slade replied before Daniel turned toward him blowing drool all over his jeans making his airplane noises. "Hey, mister!"

Daniel and Jill laughed loudly. Slade pulled him off Jill's feet and tossed him in the air, making Daniel squeal.

"This little airplane is the miracle worker." He tossed him again and Daniel squealed louder in delight.

Jill sat up and laughed. She then looked over at Duncan who still sat in the same spot he had been sitting in for the past five days, next to Pam, but this time, he was watching his son with a small smile on his face. Her eyes moved to Pam.

"Oh, my God." Jill jumped up, running toward the bed. "Pam!"

Pam looked up at Jill, her golden eyes bright. "I want to see my son," she whispered in a weak voice.

Slade hurried over, handing Daniel to Duncan. Taking their son in his arms, Duncan first leaned over, whispered something to Pam and kissed her lips softly. He then sat Daniel next to Pam, his own tears running freely down his handsome face, not caring who saw him.

Daniel reached out, touching the corner of her golden eyes. "Purty."

Jill heard sniffs, clearing of the throats and sighs, but her eyes were glued to the most beautiful sight she had ever seen. Slade took her hand leading her away and they followed everyone else out of the room to give Pam and her family their privacy.

Caroline stood next to Jax, tears wet on her cheeks. "Is she going to be okay?"

"Because of you, yes, I believe she's going to be okay." Slade reached out and squeezed her shoulder. "Thank you."

"I didn't do anything." Caroline blushed. "Daniel did it. Pam hearing her son for those two days did wonders."

"But without your insight that wouldn't have happened," Jill replied hugging Caroline. "So thank you."

Slade pulled Jill down the hall away from everyone. "I'm going to stick close because I do need to check her out after things calm down."

"Okay." Jill nodded. "I'm going to find Adam and Steve and tell them the good news."

Slade pulled her into his embrace, holding her close. "And then you rest."

"Then I rest," she agreed, but she had a lot to do and rest was the last thing on her mind. If she was going to save herself and keep Duncan from losing his position as a VC Warrior as well as going to prison, she needed to step it up.

# CHAPTER 14

Caroline sat behind Jax, loving the feel of him and the motorcycle between her legs. It was pure heaven and after the past few days, heaven was what she needed. She was exhausted beyond anything she had ever felt before, but so happy with the outcome. Now it was back to reality of getting her house together before school started in late summer.

Slowing down, Jax pulled into her driveway and Caroline actually felt a sense of home, a lonely home, but home nonetheless. Once he stopped, she slid off, feeling a little awkward. What they had been through the past five days had been intense, but this was the first they had been alone. He sent her so many mixed vibes she was afraid of showing him any of her feelings to just have them thrown back in her face.

"Thanks for bringing me home." Caroline held her bag of dirty clothes.

With ease, Jax slid off the bike and gave her a single nod. Silently, he stared at her in the way only Jax Wheeler could. He made her feel like her clothes were going to melt clean off her body and she'd be standing there completely naked. Why in the hell couldn't she be more like her sister and have plenty of witty things to say, but nope, she had to stand there like an idiot with absolutely nothing smart to say.

"Well, thanks," was the very best she could come up with. She did an about face and headed toward the house. Climbing the steps, she carefully skipped over the broken boards. Standing in front of her door, she realized she forgot the new keys for the new locks. "Well shit," she cursed, knowing that Jax was still there since she didn't hear the motorcycle start up.

"Such language for a teacher," Jax said from directly behind her making her jump a mile high.

"How in the world can you sneak up on somebody as big as you are?" Caroline peered around her shoulder to look up at him.

"You looking for these?" He dangled the keys in front of her before stepping closer, his front pressed to her back to unlock the door. "You need to keep them somewhere you won't forget them again."

Mortified that she actually leaned back into him, Caroline practically ran into the house, tripping over her own feet once he pushed open the door. Rolling her eyes at her own clumsiness, she finally turned around to face him.

"The front window doesn't lock so I can get in that way," Caroline replied without thinking.

"What?" Jax growled. He made his way to the window, locked it and gave it a try. When the window opened easily with a loud squeal, he turned to glare at her.

"Nobody knows about it but me and well, now you." Caroline crossed her arms.

"If someone wants in this…place." Jax's eyes scanned the room. "They're going to try every damn window until they find one that opens."

"And they could break it if they really wanted in," Caroline argued, thinking she made a good point.

"And that would give you time to get your gun because you will hear it," Jax countered.

"I can't get my gun because you still have it." Caroline felt pleased with herself until Jax stalked toward her like she was prey. She actually took a step back.

"Do you enjoy pushing my buttons?" Jax crowded her space.

Loaded question alert. "Do you like pushing mine?" She cocked her eyebrow and felt pretty good about standing her ground with him.

His eyes darkened as they skimmed over her from head to toe. "Most definitely." His voice was deep and dark as he stared down at her with a promise of something, but then he moved and walked right past her.

Caroline focused on the spot where Jax had been standing, before he vanished, leaving her hot and itching for his touch. He passed her again carrying a piece of wood, sticking it up in the window he measured it then broke it with his bare hands. Tossing the other piece on the ground, he wedged the piece of wood in her window, then tried to open it. Stepping back, he stared at his handiwork.

A sudden longing hit Caroline right in the gut and if she were being completely honest, in the heart also. To have a man by her side as she made this place her home—their home—was something she yearned for, and Jax Wheeler was the man she wanted it to happen with. Staring at his back, his long black hair a beautiful contrast to the white shirt he wore, she sighed.

"Do not forget your keys again." Jax turned around, catching her staring at him. "Because this window cannot be opened."

The silence was deafening. She didn't know what to say and was actually afraid to open her mouth for fear of what might come out. So instead, she nodded and turned away to do something, what she wasn't sure. This man definitely wasn't good for her mind because he turned her into a total idiot.

"The scent Hunter picked up on was a hunter." Jax continued, not realizing where her mind was.

"Oh, okay." Caroline just wished he would leave. It was so hard with him within arm's length and knowing what she wanted was so far out of her grasp.

"Which means you need to put no trespassing signs and no hunting signs on your property." Jax sounded closer.

"I'll do that." Caroline closed her eyes tightly, yearning burned in her chest.

Jax grasped her arm, turning her to face him. "Thank you for what you did."

She stared at his chest, not wanting to look into his golden eyes. "It was nothing," she replied.

"It was everything." Jax tilted her chin up with his knuckle. "And we owe you."

Caroline started to respond that no one owed her anything, but Jax held her tightly, bringing her body flush to his. She waited, not patiently, for him to kiss her again and it took everything she had not to smash her mouth against his. No, she was done doing the chasing or whatever she had been doing. If he wanted a kiss, he was going to have to take it from her.

"It seems I need to practice what I preach." Jax's eyes darkened. "I tell you to stay away from me, but I can't seem to stay away from you."

Remaining quiet seemed the smartest thing for her to do and honestly, she probably couldn't form a coherent sentence if her life depended on it. His body was hard against hers and she felt safe and protected, even though he was looking at her with a dark, dangerous stare.

His lips were inches form hers and she closed her eyes in anticipation or prayer, she didn't know which or if it was both. Finally, his lips softly touched hers, but it wasn't enough. She wanted more, dammit, and as if reading her mind, he gave her much more. His mouth ravaged hers and she savored every single minute she was in his arms and his mouth was locked to hers.

The kiss was so intense she heard banging, which was strange, but she went with it, and why was he calling her Ms. Fitzpatrick? Hell, how was he even talking? Then the kiss ended as quickly as it began. Caroline knew the disappointment on her face matched the moan of disappointment coming from her throat.

"Ms. Fitzpatrick?" The banging sound started again. "Are you okay? It's Gary from Tristate Roofing. I have your estimate and have been trying to contact you. Ms. Fitzpatrick?"

Reaching up and touching her lips, her eyes met Jax's before she glared at the door behind him.

"You want to kill him or shall I?" Jax's voice was deeper than usual with a sexual roughness that made her want to cry.

"Give me my gun back and I'll be happy to." She grumbled before heading for the door. As on and off as she and Jax were, she'd probably be an old woman before he got around to kissing her again and then she'd be too damn old for him. Grabbing the door handle at that thought, she swung the door open with force, startling Gary who jumped back with wide eyes.

"Oh, Ms. Fitzpatrick." Gary smiled, his eyes going to her lips.

For some reason him staring at her lips gave her an uncomfortable creepy feeling. Looking at the packet of papers in his hand, she reached for them. "Is that the estimate?"

"Yes," he replied, but didn't let her take it. "If you have a few minutes, I can go over everything with you."

Caroline seriously didn't have a minute, she wanted to get back inside and finish what Jax had started. "That's okay." She reached for the papers again, but he kept them out of reach. "I can look it over and then give you a call."

\*\*\*\*\*\*

Jax stood back to let Caroline handle the asshole roofer. He could see and hear everything going on from his position inside. He also had one hell of a hard-on and needed a minute. Holy shit, the woman could kiss and was hotter than anything he'd held in a long time. He had plenty of sex, but no feelings were involved, at least on his part. He just took care of his need, made sure the female was well taken care of, and on his way he went. Caroline Fitzpatrick was a whole different beautiful beast. He knew once he got her in his bed, and he was smart enough to know that would be happening sooner rather than later, no other woman would be enough for him. Deep inside in that dark area of his mind, he knew that was the reason he really wanted her to stay away from him, and not his brother; although, his brother was a serious threat.

"Jesus," he cursed, shaking his head, his eyes still on her as she talked to the roof guy. "I'm truly fucked."

When he heard the roofer guy, Gary, pressure Caroline to let him into the house to go over the estimate, he knew it was time to let the asshole know where he stood.

Stepping up behind Caroline, Jax had perverse pleasure of seeing the fear in the man's eyes. Reaching around Caroline, he grabbed the estimate and scanned it.

"Nine thousand seems pretty high." Jax frowned at the man, daring him with his eyes and attitude to try and screw Caroline over.

"Ah, well, actually…it's not." Gary cleared his throat. "The whole roof needs to be replaced and that estimate includes material plus labor."

"I'm sorry." Caroline shook her head. "I can't afford that."

Gary's whole demeanor changed. "Well, Ms. Fitzpatrick, we're very competitive with neighboring companies. You're not going to find a better deal than this."

"That doesn't change the fact that I can't afford it." Caroline frowned as she walked out into the yard and looked up at her roof. "Are you absolutely sure the whole thing needs to be replaced? I mean I know the shingles do, but the wood? There isn't any that can be saved?"

Jax knew the answer to that, but waited to see if this guy was brave enough to take advantage. He knew how these assholes worked. He would get the job, she would sign a contract, and then once he started, he would then falsely regret to inform her that more work equaling more money would have to be done. Crossing his arms over his chest, Jax waited for Gary's answer.

Glancing at Jax, Gary hurried off the porch and started pointing out things, which Jax had to give him credit were true.

"I'm sorry I've wasted your time, Gary." Caroline frowned with a sigh. "I'm going to have to go a different avenue on the roof for now."

Disappointed, Gary nodded. "I understand, but please keep my information and if you change your mind, give me a call." Gary once again glanced up to Jax, then back to Caroline. "Is that your husband?"

Caroline was still looking at the roof when Gary quietly asked her that question. "No." She frowned at him.

"Oh." Gary nodded. "Your boyfriend?"

"Gary," Jax called from the porch where he was watching and listening to every word.

Gary jumped as if guilty. "Yeah." He cautiously approached Jax.

Jax grabbed his shoulder with one hand and squeezed enough to send a message as he leaned close to his ear. "Not going to happen." Jax growled and could have sworn he heard the man gulp in fear.

Jax shoved the estimate into Gary's stomach, turned him around using his one hand on his shoulder and sent him on his way. Gary hurried to his truck without even looking at Caroline, who was still staring at her roof in despair.

It had been a long time, but it looked like Jax was going to be doing some roofing. Yeah, he was truly fucked.

# CHAPTER 15

Jill shoved two crackers in her mouth and wanted to gag. She had begun hating crackers with a passion because that was all she could eat, but it was keeping her going…kinda.

"Hey!" she yelled at Steve who was coming out of Adam's room.

Steve jumped, then turned toward her like she was a monster. "What?"

Slowing her steps, she watched Steve and knew something was up. It had been two days since Pam had pulled through, and although she found Steve to tell him the good news, she hadn't seen Adam and she really needed to talk to both him and Steve.

"Is Adam in there?" Jill went to open Adam's door, but Steve jumped in front of it, stopping her.

"He's not there." Steve's voice was a little high-pitched.

"Okay, then why were you in there?" Jill interrogated Steve, the big liar.

Steve grinned, started to say something, then frowned and grinned again. "I had to get something."

"What?" Jill cocked an eyebrow, looking at his empty hands.

"I, ah, couldn't find it." Steve, the worst liar in the world, lied.

"Cut the bullshit, Steve." Jill went to open the door, but Steve knocked her arm away.

"Angelina is naked!" Steve shouted then cringed.

Okay, that made Jill back up a step or two. "Why are you coming out of Adam's room, when he isn't there and Angelina is naked?"

Steve pursed his lips together, pointed his finger at her, and rolled his eyes to the ceiling trying his best to talk his way out of this one.

"Listen, Steve,"—Jill pushed him out of the way—"your lying is going to get you killed one day because you absolutely suck at it."

Looking over her shoulder talking to Steve about his lying, Jill opened the door to Adam's room and walked inside. When she turned around and saw Angelina holding Adam up as she was leading him to the bed, her heart sank. "Oh, Adam." Jill ran over to help Angelina. "No!"

"I'm okay," Adam replied, but didn't refuse their help. Once at the bed, he collapsed, throwing his hand over his eyes. "God, I hate throwing up."

"Steve, get Slade," Jill ordered, watching the worry flash across Angelina's face.

"I'm fine. Just give me a minute." Adam swallowed hard before peeking up at Jill then to Steve. "And dammit, Steve, I told you not to tell her."

"Dude, I didn't say a word." Steve crossed his heart. "But damn she is ruthless with her questioning."

Adam groaned and sat up quickly. "Fuck! Watch out!" Jill jumped out of the way as he ran to the bathroom with Angelina right behind him. The sound of retching echoed in the room.

"Go get Slade," Jill told Steve as they shared a look. "And then me and you need to talk."

Steve didn't question, he just ran out the door. Jill sat on the edge of the bed, her stomach cramping at the sound of Adam heaving. The feeling of defeat weaved its way into her mind, but she pushed it back and welcomed the anger. This so wasn't fair and it pissed her off.

Hearing the door open, she lifted her head, her eyes meeting Slade's.

"Where is he?" Slade asked, but then the retching started again answering his question. Slade headed that way. Angelina walked out, her face a mask of fear. Standing, Jill reached over giving her a hug. "He's going to be okay." She tried to comfort Angelina, but it sounded hollow even to her own ears.

Once Slade got Adam back on the bed, he checked him out and took his blood. "I'm going to take more blood since you're showing symptoms now. When did you feed?"

"Today," Adam replied. Jill could tell he was trying not to gag. "And I've been sick ever since."

Slade was in the process of taking his blood when Sloan entered. Jill and Steve stepped out in the hallway to give them more room. Jill pulled Steve further away.

"I need you to do something," Jill said low enough not to be overheard.

"Anything." Steve glanced at the room where more retching sounded. He looked on the verge of tears. Jill totally understood because she had been on the brink of tears for weeks.

"I need you to find out when the next City of Cincinnati council meeting is that's open to the public," Jill said, her mind going a hundred miles a minute.

"I think they're all open to the public," Steve replied, but nodded. "Okay. Yeah, I'll do it right now. What are you planning, Jill?" Steve eyed her closely.

"I'm planning on living, Steve," Jill answered. She then hugged him tightly before walking quickly away ready to set step two of her plan in motion.

*****

Two hours later, Jill stood outside of Sloan's office. She was actually getting sick of being in Sloan's office, but she couldn't chance anyone hearing what she was about to do. Taking a deep breath, she walked in closing the door behind her.

Everyone who she asked to be there was present, even Adam, who looked like hell.

"Okay, Jill," Sloan said from behind his desk. "We're all here. What do you need to say?"

Jill prayed she could do this without crying. This was her family and she was going to do everything in her power to save them. She owed it to each of them. Her eyes touched upon Damon, Jared, Duncan, Sid, Adam, and then Slade, who looked at her with a question in his gaze. Taking a deep breath, she cleared her throat.

"As you guys probably already know, Slade and I are getting married." Jill began nervously. She so didn't know how this was going to go over and she was about to pee her pants with nerves.

"Jill, honey." Sid sighed. "Are you sure you asked the right people here? I think you might be wanting to talk to the women since that's all they have been talking about."

Her phone buzzed in her back pocket. "Sorry." Jill grabbed her phone and looked at the message from Steve. Holy crap, this had better work.

"Jill." Jared frowned. "Can we please get on with this? I have something I need to do." A few grunts of agreement followed Jared's statement.

Okay, that pissed her off. "Well, excuse the hell out of me." She glared at him. "Give me a damn second, would you?"

Everyone laughed, even Adam who was looking greener by the minute.

After shooting off a text, Jill put her phone back in her pocket. "Anyway, I want to do something special, but I need you all to agree."

"Okay." Sid sighed. "What is it?"

"First agree," Jill replied, knowing it was a gamble because these

Warriors were not born yesterday and for them to agree to something without details was such a long shot. She was surprised at herself for even asking it of them.

The room erupted, everyone talking to her at once. Jill's shoulders slumped from the onslaught, but her eyes caught Duncan's who wasn't saying a word, just staring at her as if reading her, but she knew that wasn't happening because she was closed off tight.

"I agree." Duncan's voice boomed above everyone.

Tears tickled the back of Jill's eyes, but she held them back. "Thank you," she said to Duncan before looking at the others.

"Ah, what the hell." Jared sighed. "I agree."

Soon the whole room agreed and Jill knew for a fact she was going to fight for these men and their loved ones if it was the last thing she did, and it probably would be the last thing she did.

"I know you all love your mates above anything." Grunts of agreements followed her statement. "I want my wedding to be your wedding also."

"Let me get this straight." Sid scratched his chin. "You want us all to get married at the same time?"

"Yes." Jill nodded, then looked at Damon. "Damon, you and Nicole could renew your vows along with all of us."

No one said anything else. The room was silent. Her worried eyes met Slade's and wondered if he was upset, but his widening smile and nod of approval made her heart soar.

"But there is one stipulation," Jill added. This is where it was going to get tricky. "It has to be in a week and I don't want the women to know. I want it to be a surprise. The only thing you have to do is make sure they are at the place I tell you and you get the rings and a tux."

Again the room was silent until Damon spoke up. "Why a week and why a surprise?"

"The surprise is because this is something I want to do for my sisters." Jill felt the lump in her throat growing. "I want this day to be special, not only for me, but for them and you guys as well. It's the only gift I can give to them for everything they've done for me. And as for the timeframe, I think we all know the answer to that." Her eyes met Adam's.

"You've given a lot of thought to this." Jared observed, a soft expression on his face.

"Yes," she lied, unless two days was a lot of thought.

"Any of the unmated males along with Blaze and Hunter could give someone away. My dad will be giving me away." Jill looked around at everyone staring at her. "I'll give you more information in the next day or two."

"What do you need from me?" Sloan asked, an approving gleam in his eyes.

Jill's eyes met Duncan's briefly. "Don't turn Duncan in."

"He doesn't have a choice," Duncan replied before Sloan could. "I would turn myself in if he didn't. I will not bring down my brothers that way. It's the law and VC Warriors uphold the law, always."

"Even bullshit laws?" Jill said in disgust, but didn't expect anyone to answer. "Okay, fair enough."

"Anything else?" Sloan replied with a small grin.

"An advance on my paycheck?" Jill cringed when she asked the other question she'd been dreading. Then smiled when Sloan nodded with a laugh.

As each Warrior left the room, they hugged Jill. Adam, other than Slade, was the last. "You are crazy." Adam hugged her, but his eyes told her how much he appreciated her thoughtfulness.

"That's no secret." Jill laughed, hugging him again. "Now go take care of yourself."

She watched him walk slowly out of the room, which was not at all Adam like. He was hurting and it scared her. Time was definitely not on their side. Her eyes swung back to Slade who stood in the corner of the room watching her.

"Please don't be upset." Jill kind of regretted not asking Slade since this was his day also, but she couldn't chance him saying no.

Pushing himself off the wall, he walked to her, taking her in his arms and kissing her slowly. "I love you more than I ever thought possible." He held her close.

"Thank you." Jill hugged him back.

"For what?" He pulled back looking down at her.

"For loving me." Jill kissed his chin.

"What do you need me to help you with?" Slade brushed his thumb across her cheek.

"Just show up." Jill smiled up at him and kissed his palm.

"I wouldn't miss it for the world." He pressed his lips against hers.

"Oh, and I need to borrow your car." Jill stepped away holding out her hand. "With Adam sick, I'd feel guilty stealing his car."

Slade's eyes narrowed, but he placed the keys in her hand. "You need to take it easy, Jill," Slade warned. "The crackers and Pepsi may be working for you now, but—"

"I'm getting plenty of rest, Slade. I promise." She chauffeured him toward the door. "Now go check on Adam. He looked pretty green when he left. I'm fine."

Jill watched Slade leave before grabbing her phone. Looking up the number she needed, she hit send and waited. "Hey, I need your help." Jill smiled. "Thank you. Text me your address. I'll be there in half an hour."

Jill pumped her arm in the air in excitement mixed with a little relief. Turning, she headed for the door when a wave of dizziness hit her.

"Whoa." She grabbed onto the doorframe. "Slow down, dumbass." Taking deep calming breaths, she opened her eyes to see if the dizziness subsided. Feeling more stable, Jill headed out being more cautious and slowing the hell down.

# CHAPTER 16

Jill pulled into the long driveway and stopped alongside Hunter, who was nailing a sign to a wooden post. "Hey," Jill called out, leaning toward the passenger side window. "You need a ride?"

Hunter stepped back to look at his handiwork before turning and jumping in the car. "It's hotter than hell out there." He looked over at her with a grin. "What are you up to?"

"I came to see Caroline." Jill drove slowly down the bumpy driveway. "What about you?" She glanced at the hammer in his hand.

"There's been some hunters on Caroline's property so Jax wanted me to go around posting these signs." Hunter held up a No Trespassing sign. "Yeah, the big bad shifter comes up from the hills of Kentucky to hang signs."

Jill grinned. "Nothing on Jax's brother I take it?"

"Not even a lead." Hunter's brow furrowed in disappointment.

"You going to be staying around long?" Jill parked, taking the keys out of the ignition.

He got out of the car and pushed the door closed. "Probably for another week or two, unless something comes up."

Following him to the front door, Jill got her first good look at Caroline's new house. "Wow."

Hunter glanced over at her with a smirk. "That's one way of looking at it."

"This place is awesome." Jill looked around in awe.

"Are you blind?" Hunter eyed her as if she were nuts.

"Hey!" Caroline walked out of the house with Jax following close behind.

"Caroline, this place is beautiful." Jill ignored Hunter and climbed the wooden steps, missing the broken one.

Jax and Hunter both looked at the house confused, then at each other.

"Thank you." Caroline smiled with pride. "It needs a lot of work, but I love it."

"Okay, wait a minute." Hunter held up his hands shaking his head. "Are you both out of your ever-loving minds? Caroline, I really like you… I do, but this place is a dump."

"No, it's not!" Jill defended, both women glaring at him. "I mean, it does need a lot of work, but you need to look past that and see the beauty."

Hunter took two steps back and stared at the house for a long minute. "Nope, don't see it."

"Well, you don't need to see it." Caroline frowned. "Because you didn't buy it…"

"Thank God." Hunter snorted.

"I did and it's mine and it's beautiful." Caroline ignored his snide comment.

"If it doesn't have a beer or boobs, they'll never get it." Jill rolled her eyes at a grinning Jax and followed Caroline inside.

"That *would* be a definite improvement," Hunter called after them.

"Ignore him." Jill looked around. "This place will be a dream when you're finished."

Caroline nodded in agreement. "I'm really excited and a little nervous."

Jill looked over her shoulder at Jax, who had stayed outside. "Well, it seems you have plenty of help." She glanced back at Caroline with a cocked eyebrow.

Blushing, Caroline was also looking at Jax, but totally skimmed over Jill's statement. "So what's going on?"

A wave of dizziness hit Jill making her squeeze her eyes shut to stop the room from spinning around her.

"Jill?" Caroline grabbed her.

"I'm okay. It'll pass." Jill took a deep calming breath, but she did grab onto Caroline's arm.

"You need to be resting." Jax, hearing Caroline's worried voice, came back inside the house.

"You sound like Slade." Jill snorted as she opened her eyes slowly. "And I don't have time to rest."

Jax had pulled out his phone, but didn't make the call as he stood staring down at her.

"You guys need to promise me that what I'm about to tell you will stay here." Jill looked at them both. She wasn't planning on saying anything in front of Jax, but knew he wasn't going to go anywhere and, in the end, she was going to need his help. Knowing Hunter was on the porch also listening, she added, "That includes you, wolfie."

Hunter strolled in with Blaze following him. "Wolfie?

That's a good one." Blaze laughed as he walked past Jill and placed the signs and a hammer down on the table. "Signs are posted all along the back of the property," he informed Jax, still wearing a huge grin.

"If you don't want my 'wolfie' biting your ass, you will never call me that again," Hunter warned everyone in the room with a glare.

"That totally depends on what you tell us." Jax ignored Hunter. "And until I know what it is, I promise nothing."

Jill stared at him for a long second before sighing. "There's going to be a huge wedding…"

"Oh, I know." Caroline smiled. "I can't wait for you and Slade—"

"It's not just me and Slade." Jill stopped her, wanting to get this over with because she was feeling dizzy again. Spotting a chair, she weaved herself to it. Blaze actually steadied her until she sat down.

"I'm calling Slade." Jax started hitting numbers on his phone.

"Please!" Jill cried out. "Don't."

Jax looked up from his phone, a worry creasing his brow. "Jill…"

"I'm fine," Jill said with irritation. "I'm fine!" she repeated louder, her voice cracking.

Hunter and Blaze shared a look, but Jill ignored it. Her eyes shot back to Jax with a plea that couldn't be missed.

"Jax." Caroline shook her head.

Putting his phone away, he frowned. "I won't call Slade, yet," Jax stated. "But I'm not letting you out of my sight until you're back with him."

Jill nodded, too damn tired to argue. She had to get her plan set in motion and soon. "I've asked Damon, Jared, Sid, Duncan, and Adam if they would share this day with me and Slade. They agreed. Damon and Nicole are already married, but they are going to renew their vows."

Caroline slapped her hand over her mouth with excitement. "Oh, Jill, that is…" This time, it was Caroline's voice cracking as her eyes filled with happy tears. "Lana and Sid are getting married. I've got to call her."

"You can't." Jill shook her head. "Lana doesn't know. None of them know."

"What?" everyone in the room said at the same time.

"It's something I want to do for them because of how they've treated me. They're my sisters," Jill replied, leaving out the other reason…for now. "And I need your help to pull this off."

All four of them were looking at her as if she'd lost her mind. Caroline was the first to speak. "You know I'll help. So when's the wedding?" Caroline laughed, almost bouncing up and down. "Weddings?" she corrected herself.

"A week from today." Jill stood when everyone started talking at once, except for Jax who just stared at her as if he saw right through her.

"A week!" Caroline gasped. "Jill, how in the world is that going to happen?"

"Adam's sick now." Just saying those words made her stomach twist painfully. "It will happen and in a week."

"Fuck!" Understanding flashed across Jax's face.

******

Caroline stared out the window, so many emotions swirling through her body. She peeked in the backseat where Jill sat with her head tilted back, eyes closed. Her eyes met Jax's, but they remained silent. The whole time Jill had been inside her house, the little dead boy had been by Jill's side, his small face staring up at her, and Caroline knew what that meant. She and Lana had learned that when a spirit attached itself to someone who was sick, they were waiting to guide them into the afterlife. Jill's time was limited and it broke her heart.

Caroline now understood Jill's haste in pushing the wedding forward. Jill had given them all orders any leader would be proud of. She was precise in what needed to be done, down to what each woman would wear, including their dress sizes, shocking Caroline that Jill had done so much research. A sneaky smile had spread across Jill's lips before she explained that the women had already been sized for their bridesmaid dresses. Instead of bridesmaid dresses, Caroline was to pick out simple wedding dresses for each.

A dog barking brought Caroline out of her thoughts. A huge black German shepherd stood outside Jax's window.

"Sable," Jill said, her voice groggy with sleep.

Another smaller dog joined in, barking excitedly as Jill opened the door. Jax climbed out, as did Caroline, hoping to God the huge black dog didn't attack her. Walking around the car, she knew her fear was unfounded when both dogs excitedly welcomed Jill home.

"Hey!" Jill laughed, giving each dog attention. "I've missed you, too." Jill accepted the licks each dog happily gave.

When the large dog became too excited jumping up on Jill and bumping her into the car, Jax whistled loudly, snapped his fingers, and pointed to the ground. Both dogs stopped immediately. Their eyes traveled to Jax, but their tails still went a hundred miles an hour.

"That was impressive." Caroline looked up at Jax in surprise. "Would that work with Hunter?"

Jax glanced over at her with a huge grin. "I don't know." He chuckled. "I'll have to try it."

Caroline laughed. "I want to see that."

"Jilly!" A young boy slammed open the front door and ran at breakneck speed down the steps. Throwing himself into Jill's arms, he knocked her on her ass from her kneeling position near the dogs.

The dogs wanted to join, but Jax growled and they remained sitting, panting with their tails wagging in excitement.

"Oh, my God." Jill held the little boy out from her. "You can't be Seth."

"I am," he said proudly, puffing his little chest out.

"You can't be," Jill continued to tease. "You're too big to be my little Seth."

"Jilly, it's me," Seth said, his tone turning worried.

Jill laughed, hugging her brother tightly. "I know that silly." She tickled his stomach. "I was just teasing you. Is Mom and Dad here?"

Caroline grinned as she watched Jill and her little brother, but her heart also ached.

"What do you want, Jillian?" A woman's voice came out of nowhere. Caroline looked around Jax to see a beautiful woman walking their way.

Jill stood, helping Seth up. "I needed to talk to you and Dad," Jill replied, and then glanced uncomfortably at Jax and Caroline. "These are my friends, Jax and Caroline. This is my mom."

"It's nice to meet you, Mrs. Nichols." Caroline smiled, feeling uncomfortable when Jill's mom seemed to study her and found her lacking. Jax didn't say a word. He remained standing with arms crossed, staring ahead.

Trevor picked that moment to come flying down the driveway breaking the uncomfortable situation.

"Can you give a guy some warning, Jill?" Trevor hopped out of the car. "I had a hot date waiting for me, but you threatening me with bodily harm if I didn't show up here ruined the mood."

"I've seen some of your dates, Trevor. And believe me their not as hot as you think they are." Jill shot back with a roll of her eyes, Caroline snorted, Jax grinned, while Seth climbed up on Trevor's back, and their mom narrowed her eyes in disapproval.

"I have to disagree, sister. Busty Barb is as hot as they come." Trevor smiled a hello to Jax and Caroline. "Okay, can we get this show on the road so I can get some action going without fear of getting my ass kicked?"

"Trevor!" her mom scolded with a slight shake of her head. Everyone grinned, even Ms. Nichols who seemed to have relaxed a little.

# CHAPTER 17

Jill watched her mom trying her best not to smile as Seth continued to say ass, but then she had to become stern to make him stop. Jill just stood there as Trevor headed toward the house, followed by her mom. She hadn't been in her home since the day she'd been turned. Trevor stopped at the steps looking back at her.

"Well, are you coming?" Trevor frowned. Seth was still on his back, but silent.

Glancing at Jax and Caroline, she saw that they were staring at her, waiting for her cue. Making her feet move, she followed Trevor up the steps. Her mom had already gone inside. At the door, she paused before going inside.

"Are you okay?" Jax leaned down to whisper to her.

Jill nodded. "Just been a long time since I've been welcomed here," she replied honestly.

Even before she stepped inside, the smells of home hit her hard. Her eyes traveled the room. Overwhelmed with memories, her knees weakened. Nothing had changed. The door they went through led into the kitchen, which was still painted in the same pale yellow. Her gaze automatically went to the white lace curtains that she had always loved. Finally, her eyes met her mother's, and there was something there other than fear and disdain.

"Jelly Bean!" Her dad walked into the kitchen, his hair a little messy indicating he'd been napping, probably in the same old chair he had since she was a child.

"Hey, Dad!" Jill swallowed the large lump stuck in the back of her throat. She walked over, hugged him tightly, and then smoothed his hair down like she used to do. "You taking care of yourself?"

"Well, you just caught me napping in the middle of the day. I'd say that's taking care of myself pretty darn good." He chuckled then looked toward Jax and Caroline.

"Dad, this is Jax Wheeler and Caroline Fitzpatrick," Jill introduced them, glancing at her mother again, but she had since busied herself with Seth.

"Nice meeting you, Mr. Nichols." Caroline smiled, taking his hand.

"Call me Chuck." He shook her hand then Jax's with a large friendly smile. "Where's Slade?"

"He's taking care of some things," Jill replied, having a hard time looking him in the eyes. She was full of nervous energy making her fidget, and she knew how much her mother hated when she fidgeted. "I needed to talk to you and Mom about something."

"Well, come on in and have a seat." Chuck ushered them further into the kitchen. Everyone sat but Trevor and Jax. "Anyone want something to drink? We've got water, soda...beer." That last was directed toward Jax.

"No, thank you," Jax and Caroline both declined.

All attention turned toward her. Clearing her throat, she looked at her mom before beginning. "I'm supposed to get married in three weeks." She glanced at her dad who was nodding. Of course he knew; he was walking her down the aisle. "We've changed the date to Saturday."

"This Saturday?" Her father's eyes opened in surprise.

"Yes, and I don't want to get married in a church," Jill replied and then took a deep breath. "I want to get married here, in the woods. In the clearing." In her special place, she thought, but didn't say that aloud. "You and Mom will have to do nothing except be here. I'm taking care of everything with the help of friends."

The room was silent and Jill felt the hope of them saying yes slowly dwindle away.

"Well, I don't know about you guys, but I think that's a awesome idea. And after they say their 'I dos' they can run down the dirt aisle, grab the vine and do a double backflip into the lake to seal the deal." Trevor's smile was huge. He winked at Jill.

"Before you answer, I need to tell you it won't just be me and Slade. There will be five other couples. Vampire and human," Jill added, then held her breath.

"This is your home, Jill." Her dad's voice shook slightly. "Of course you can get married here."

Jill gave her dad a loving smile, trying her best to hold her tears in. "Thank you, Dad." Her eyes went to her mom. "But I need Mom to agree also."

Her mom stood as still as stone staring at Jill. "Are you sick?" Her mother's voice also shook.

"What?" Her dad's eyes widened. "Sick? Jill isn't sick."

"I saw something on the news saying…" Her mother didn't finish. Her gaze never faltered as she stared at Jill.

Jill reached over and grabbed her dad's hand before answering. "Yes, I'm sick."

Her mom said nothing, just turned, and walked out of the room.

Standing, Jill hugged her dad. "I'm going to be okay, Dad." She leaned down and kissed his shocked face. "Slade is working hard to find out what's wrong, so please don't worry."

"I'm your father," he replied, kissing her cheek. "I'll always worry, but I know that young man of yours won't let anything happen to you."

Jill straightened and went to walk out of the room. "I'll be right back," Jill told Caroline and Jax as she passed. Making her way through the house, Jill couldn't help but look around, not only looking for her mom, but searching for the memories as she passed them by. Stopping in front of her parents' bedroom, she looked inside. Her mother stood with her back facing the door.

"I don't hate you, Jillian." Her mother's voice sounded tired and worn down. Her shoulders were slumped. Turning, she looked at Jill, her eyes moist with tears before walking to the closet and digging something out from the back. Her mom placed a box on the bed, lifting the lid.

Gazing at the box, Jill's whole world shifted. Everything from a pair of baby shoes, drawings she had created, to school reports lay perfectly placed inside the box. She was speechless.

Her mom walked around the bed and took her hand, leading her out of the room and up the stairs. She opened the attic door. Even though Jill feared this room with a passion because Trevor, the ass, told her the boogeyman lived in there, Jill followed her mother inside.

"That is all your stuff." Her mother pointed to boxes stacked in one corner.

"But I thought…" Jill looked at her, confused.

Her mother didn't let her finish as she pulled her out of the attic and down the hall to her old room. She opened the door and pulled Jill inside. Nothing had changed. Her bed was under the window, her desk still sat in the same place, as did her dresser.

"Trevor said you and Janie threw my things out."

Her mother swallowed visibly. "Trevor was devastated when you went missing, and then when you came back and left again, he blamed me."

Jill wanted to say it was her fault that she left home, but she stayed silent.

"And I didn't correct him." Her mother actually looked ashamed.

Jill walked over and opened her closet. All her clothes were gone. She turned to look at her mom.

"In the boxes in the attic," her mother answered Jill's unspoken question. "That's what we were doing that night."

"Why?" Jill shook her head, unsure which question she had for her mother to answer first. *Why*, seemed like the best place to start.

"I never knew how to help you, Jillian," her mother replied.

"By being my mother." Hot blinding anger made her heart beat faster, but she did her best to keep the attitude out of her tone. "That's all I wanted. I felt like a burden because I had a reading disability."

"I didn't know how to help you, so I ignored you and brushed the problem aside." Her eyes never flickered from Jill's. "I failed you in every way a mother could fail her child."

Feeling weak, Jill walked over and sat on the edge of her bed. "And then I came home a monster."

Her mother wiped the tear that leaked from her eye, but didn't answer. "I'm sorry." Those two words her mother spoke rang true.

Looking away from her mother, Jill's eyes roamed her room, seeing everything that once made her who she was. All her drawings were still taped to the light blue walls of her room. A weird sense of wanting to laugh filled her soul. She was finally getting what she wanted from her mother, yet she was dying. Lowering her head, Jill looked at the floor she had laid upon doing drawing after drawing. Tears spilled from her eyes, some clear, others red. Her chest hurt so badly, she thought that this may be it—she was going to die right there in the room she spent so many hours hoping, dreaming…wanting her mother's approval, her love. A laugh mixed with a sob escaped her throat.

"You can have your wedding here with your friends, Jillian." Her mother's voice broke through her meltdown.

Hearing her mother's footsteps moving past her, Jill raised her head, stood and pulled her mother into a hug. She couldn't say anything except cry. And she cried even harder when her mom held her just as tightly, her own body shaking in sobs.

"I know I can never ask you to forgive me, Jillian. I will never be able to forgive myself," her mother said against her shoulder. "Just know I'm so sorry."

"I've already forgiven you. All I've ever wanted was your love, your acceptance." Jill sobbed right back. Jill pulled back to look at her mom, a sob escaping her throat and ending in a laugh. "We're a mess." Her mom did the same, laughing on her own sob.

"Jilly, Shade's here." Seth's small voice broke through their laughing and crying.

"You mean Slade?" Jill corrected him with a grin. Letting go of her mom, she wiped her face.

"Yeah, that's what I said," Seth frowned. "Why are you crying, Momma?"

"Because I'm happy." Jill's mom also wiped her face.

Jill hoped her face was clean of blood before turning around. She didn't want to scare Seth. Her mom actually reached up and wiped her cheek. She then nodded, which made Jill well up again. Fighting back the tears, she turned. Seth stood in the doorway, his little hand in Slade's big one.

Slade didn't say a word, but his eyes spoke volumes. All Jill could manage was a nod because if she opened her mouth, she was going to lose it again.

Jill's mom walked around Jill and stood in front of Slade. "I want to apologize for the way I treated you."

"It doesn't matter how you treat me, ma'am." Slade looked down at the woman. "Jill's my concern and how she's treated."

"Fair enough, but I still apologize." She grabbed Seth's hand. "And please, call me Ruth."

Slade stepped to the side so she and Seth could pass. He then headed directly for Jill.

"Why are you here?" she asked and then grinned at his cocked eyebrow. "I didn't mean that the way it sounded, *Shade*," she teased with the name Seth gave him.

"I'm here because Jax texted me worried about you." Slade frowned. He reached up, touching her cheek then forehead. "How are you feeling?"

Jill started to lie, but knew he would know so she sighed. "I'm okay, just really shaky and weak. You know, the usual." She tried to tease, but fell way short of being funny. "Do you think you can try the transfusion on…?"

"No!" There was absolutely no give in his voice. With that single answer, the subject was closed. "I would change you first."

"Not if it gets you put in jail, or makes you lose your VC status and medical license you won't," Jill replied with a no give tone to her own voice, but Slade didn't seem impressed. Instead, he glared before looking around her room.

"So, this is Jillian Nichols' room." Slade walked over to the wall looking at her drawings. "You are very talented."

"Thanks." Jill smiled with pride. "This is probably one of my favorites, other than the one I drew of you." She pointed to one of Sable and Bebe.

"Are you sorry?" Slade asked without looking at her; he continued to look at the pictures.

"About what?" Jill frowned, hearing the emotion he was trying to hide in his voice. When he didn't answer, she grabbed his arm and turned him to face her. "Sorry about what?"

"That you were turned." His eyes searched hers, looking for the truth.

"If you would have asked me that after it happened, then yes." Jill wrapped her arms around his waist. "But the day you showed up and shoved Jeff's face in the concrete changed that completely. So no, Slade, I'm not sorry because I would have never met you."

# CHAPTER 18

Once again, Jill found herself sitting alone in the kitchen. It had been three days since she had been at her parents' house and the miracle of all miracles had happened with her mother. They had actually exchanged cell phone numbers and to her surprise her mother was a *huge* texter. She didn't know if her sickness had changed her mom's feelings, but she didn't care. Life was too short. Even though, ironically for her it was supposed to be long, but that didn't seem to be the case now.

Some would see her acceptance of her mom's apology as something she should decline, but Jill loved and had always loved her mother, and this was a new beginning for them. In a weird kind of way, she understood her mother's fear, and that was all that mattered. No one else's opinion, other than Slade's, mattered to her.

So far everything seemed to be going smoothly, and she smiled taking another bite of a cracker, the smile disappearing in a disgusted grimace.

"Taste like shit, don't they?" Adam sat down across from her at the table. He grabbed a cracker shoving it in his mouth. "Why couldn't we be able to stomach steak instead of fucking crackers?"

"Or blood." Jill sighed, taking a sip of warm Pepsi.

"God, I'm so thirsty." Adam grabbed her Pepsi and took a swig. "But not for this shit. I feel like I'm slowly starving, Jill."

"I know." Jill's heart flipped and not in a good way. What he said was absolutely true. They were slowly starving to death. Without blood, they wouldn't survive.

"Angelina is so afraid and I don't know what to do, what to tell her." Adam's voice shook with emotion to the point where he cleared his throat. "Has Slade found out anything at all?"

"No." Jill wished she could tell him something different, but she wasn't going to lie. "I think he's just waiting to turn me, but I'm not letting that happen unless the laws change."

"So you'd rather die than let Slade change you?" Adam stared at her as if trying to understand.

"Slade's a doctor, a VC Warrior, it would ruin him to change me," Jill responded firmly. "I can't live with knowing I was his downfall."

Adam started to say something but Sloan walked in the room holding something in his hand. "Been looking for you." He handed her a check. "Sorry it took me so long, that should cover whatever's needed."

Jill looked at the check and about choked on the cracker she had just put in her mouth. "This is too much." Jill handed it back to him, but then pulled it back looking at it. "Exactly how much do I get paid anyway?"

Sloan's lips curved up in a half grin. "Only part of that is your pay advance. The guys pitched in to pay for their part."

"That wasn't the deal." Jill frowned again, handing the check back, which he wouldn't take.

"They figured you'd say that and said to tell you that this is the deal, and if you didn't accept it, then the weddings were off." Sloan replied, then walked out before Jill could argue further.

"How much is it?" Adam plucked it out of her fingers to look at it. "Holy shit. Can I borrow a couple thousand?" He gave her a 'pretty please' smile.

Jill stood, plucking it right back out of his fingers. "Not a chance." She grinned and headed out of the kitchen.

As she made her way to her room, she had to watch for any of the girls. She told everyone else to keep the secret, but she totally sucked at secrets. That was why she was sneaking down the halls as if she were on some covert operation with the VC Warriors. Rushing inside her room, she shut the door. Slade walked out of the bathroom totally naked drying his hair with a towel.

"Good thing it was me." Her eyes roamed his body and a sudden heat flushed across her skin.

Slade's smile was slow, his eyes roaming over her. It had been way too long since he had touched her and she knew exactly why. She turned away from him and gazed at herself in the mirror, something she tried not to do lately. Her cheeks were sunken as were her eyes, which looked flat. The paleness of her skin made the shadows under her mismatched eyes even more pronounced. Steve was right; she looked like shit. Closing her eyes, she shut out the truth of the situation staring back at her.

"Open your eyes," Slade said from directly behind her. His heat surrounded her.

Jill did as he said, but looked up over her head to stare at him, not her reflection. "I know why you haven't touched me." Jill didn't take her eyes off him. "I can't blame you. Steve's right, I look like shit."

Turning her around, Slade glared down at her. "Steve's a fucking idiot." Slade raised an eyebrow as if emphasizing that fact. "And I'm taking it slow with you until you're stronger."

"Don't lie to me, Slade." Jill tried to look away, but he wouldn't let her. "I would totally understand if you want to call off our wedding."

"Jill, I'm going to marry you because that is what I want." Slade's voice turned into a growl.

"I'm gross," Jill replied, then laughed at her choice of words, despite her eyes misting with tears.

Slade didn't laugh. "You are the most beautiful woman I've ever seen."

"You have to say that." Jill rolled her eyes.

"No." Slade's voice held conviction. "I don't. I just know exactly what will put you in jeopardy and as badly as I want to lay you down underneath me at this very moment, it's not going to happen. It's not worth the risk."

"So is this what it's going to be like being married to a doctor?" Jill grumbled, but her heart felt a little lighter. "I get a little sniffle and…"

"This is not a little sniffle and you know it." Slade had already put on a pair of slacks and reached over grabbing a shirt.

She sighed and then eyed him. "Where you going?"

"To get my tux with the rest of the men you and Caroline have been ordering around." He winked at her. Leaning down, he kissed her softly. "I cannot wait to make you my wife. I love you."

Jill kissed him back with a tight hug. "I love you."

"Now rest for a while and I'll be back soon." Slade smiled. Something flickered in his eyes, but was gone as soon as it appeared.

As the door closed, Jill felt more alone than she ever had and she knew it was fear making her feel this way. She could yell right now and Slade would be in front of her in two seconds flat. Glancing at the closed door, she thought about doing just that but didn't. She'd be damned if she let fear win. She was stronger than that.

******

Slade went the opposite way of the game room, where he was supposed to meet the guys, past his office and out the door to the parking lot. He continued until he knew he was out of sight of the cameras. Stopping, he just stood, staring at nothing. With his hands clenched at his sides, his body pulsed in rage. It took every ounce of discipline he possessed not to show any negative emotion around Jill, around any of them. He was their doctor. He should be able to do something except watch the woman he loved slowly starving to death in front of his fucking eyes.

Tilting his head back, he held back the roar he felt building in his chest. Afraid if he let go, he would be too far gone in his rage to return to the man he needed to be for Jill. All his life he had waited for her, though he didn't know it until he had seen her that first day playing tag football, and still he had tried to fight it. Flashes of memories filtered through his brain as he stood, head back with his eyes closed.

Jill's words came back to him like a punch in the gut. For her to even think for one minute that he didn't want to marry her, make love to her, told him he was failing miserably at taking care of her. For Jill to have any doubts of his devotion to her was unacceptable. His insides twisted at the mere thought of not having her in his life, so why in the hell did he have such a hard time expressing that to her? Just the thought of losing Jill brought his rage even closer.

His eyes opened, black as night as he stared toward the sky. "I will not lose her." His voice was hoarse with emotion. Bringing his head down he wasn't surprised at the wetness on his face. Determination and rage filled his soul as did the love for his mate. "I *will not* fail her."

Turning, he swiped his face before heading back inside, feeling a little more in control. He grabbed the door handle and swung the door open.

"Fuck!" Steve jumped back with a squeal. "I think I just shit my pants."

Slade didn't say a word as he passed Steve.

"They're all waiting for you and sent me to find you." Steve walked fast to keep up with Slade. Then almost ran smack into him when Slade slowed by the door to his room, but then kept going.

Making it to the game room, Slade stepped inside, his eyes finding Sloan. "I'm turning her after the wedding."

Sloan didn't say anything for a second, but of course, Steve did.

"You can't!" Steve said a little too fast. When everyone looked at him, he shuffled his feet nervously. "I mean, she'll be mad. She doesn't want you to turn her. Can't somebody else maybe later next week or something."

"Later next week?" Slade tilted his head, his eyes narrowing at Steve. "Why later next week?"

"Ah, well…" Everyone in the room knew Steve was hiding something. He knew they knew which made him a nervous mess. "Because…I mean instead of you changing her, someone else can."

"No one will touch her." Slade's growl rattled the room, his body stiffened as if ready to attack.

"Let's keep calm, Slade." Jared placed himself between Steve and Slade. "Steve's just talking out his ass again."

"Yeah." Steve's voice was full of relief as he peeked around Jared to Slade. "I do that a lot…talking out my ass. I'm an ass talker for sure. I even—"

"Steve." Sid coughed, shaking his head and mimicking a cutting motion across his neck indicating to Steve he needed to shut the fuck up.

Slade's glare went back to Sloan, then to Adam. "I'll change Adam also."

Adam, who was sitting slumped in a chair, looked up. "I'm good, man." His voice was weak.

Nothing about Adam was good; they all knew it. He was deteriorating fast.

"I'll change Adam," Duncan said from his place against the pool table.

"Yeah, and have two counts against you." Sloan shook his head. "No. How much time do we have, Slade?"

Slade stared at Sloan before looking at Adam then at nothing but empty space. "Not long."

"We're not losing anyone," Sloan said, anger lacing every word. "Let's get this wedding shit over with and set a plan into action. If anyone needs to be turned before then, they *will* be turned and we'll deal with the consequences later."

"I wouldn't let Jill hear you call the wedding…wedding shit," Steve added, not knowing when to shut the hell up. "Just sayin'."

"The kid's got a point." Sid laughed. "Now let's get this over with. Caroline's going to meet us and take tuxes to Jill's parents' house."

Slade watched each of his brothers leave the room until just he and Sloan remained. "I've been talking to my colleagues in California," Slade said, his eyes darkening. "They've tried to get the law changed there and it's been shut down. They've lost over fifty half-breeds and that's only in their area. We have no idea how many have died across the country. They are keeping this quiet, just a few leaks from the media. The government is doing everything in their power to make sure the human race does not become outnumbered by vampires."

Sloan cursed. "Have they been given the same serum as Pam, Jill, and Adam?"

"There's no way to tell." Slade's voice deepened in anger. "We need to find out who's making this shit and put a stop to it."

"Well, if I lose my Warriors that isn't going to happen," Sloan replied, then slapped Slade on the back. "But I understand what you need to do because if it were me, I wouldn't hesitate to change my mate if it needed to be done."

Surprised, Slade looked at Sloan as they headed out the door.

"And if you tell any one of those sons of bitches out there I said that I will kill you." Sloan gave him a warning glance before walking out of the room. "I don't need fucking Sid or Jared matchmaking."

Slade followed him out, shaking his head with a small smile that didn't reach his eyes. There was no happiness in his soul until Jill was safe.

# CHAPTER 19

The day had finally arrived and Caroline was about to have a full-blown panic attack. Trying to pull off a wedding in one week with six brides and grooms was just crazy, but there she was right smack in the middle of it. The few guests who had been invited were mingling in the woods with the tux-clad Warriors, and that alone was a heart-stopping moment for any hot-blooded woman. Poor Trevor and Steve had been hiding cars for an hour. Everyone invited knew what was going on and were more than happy to be a part of the surprise.

"Breathe," Jax said from behind her. "Everything is perfect. You've done an amazing job."

Caroline frowned as she continued to look around. "Are you sure? I feel like I'm missing something." The clearing was set up with chairs decorated with green vines and flowers. White lights were strung through the trees and the archway that Jax, Hunter, and Blaze made for the occasion was gorgeous.

"It's fine." Jax smiled down at her nervous frown.

"I just don't want Jill to be disappointed." She worried her bottom lip with her teeth.

Jax groaned before tugging her arm. "Come on. You need to get up to the house before the women show up or they're going to catch you coming out of the woods."

Caroline let Jax lead her, but kept turning around looking at the clearing until they turned the bend and she couldn't see the beautiful wedding setup anymore. They stayed to the side of the white runner the brides would walk on along the trail.

Trevor and Steve met them, keeping clear of the white runner since Caroline threatened bodily harm if they stepped foot on it.

"Cars are hidden." Steve gave her a thumbs up.

"And let me tell you it wasn't easy," Trevor grumbled but smiled.

"Although, that Mustang GT was freaking awesome. I think I parked that one farthest away."

"Dude, that's Damon's car," Steve said as they headed down the trail where everyone was. "You better hope nothing happens to it 'cause that mean son of a bitch decapitates people who piss him off."

"Ah, come on." Trevor snorted.

"I shit you not…" Steve's voice trailed off as they disappeared around the bend.

Caroline grinned, shaking her head. "Okay, well, I guess I'll see you later."

Jax nodded, his eyes never leaving hers.

"Ah, well, okay." God, she sounded like an idiot, but Jax Wheeler in a tux could make any woman act like a complete fool. She turned, started toward the house, and then stopped. "Oh, I'll text you when we're ready for the ushers."

Again Jax nodded, but this time, a small grin tugged the corner of his mouth.

"Yeah, okay." Caroline turned back around, rolling her eyes at herself. She could feel his eyes on her as she made her way across the yard and prayed she didn't trip. Secretly, she hoped her ass looked good in her jeans. "Jesus, Caroline. Stop being such a slut." The deep chuckle behind her sent a burning flush up her neck to her face. Lord, she just needed to keep her mouth shut around that man.

Opening the door to the house, Caroline headed upstairs where she knocked on Jill's door. "Come in."

Jill sat in front of a mirror while her mom styled her hair. Caroline really didn't know how she felt about Ruth Nichols. The stories she'd heard about her and Jill's relationship didn't sit well, but Jill seemed happy and that was what counted, especially today.

"Is everything ready?" Jill turned to look at Caroline, excitement and a strange sadness in her eyes.

"It's perfect." Caroline replied, praying that Jill would think so. "All the guys are there, know what to do, and are ready to go."

"Are the girls here yet?" Jill stood, hugging her robe tightly against her body. She stumbled as she stood, then sat back down quickly.

Looking away from Jill, Caroline checked her watch. "No, but they will be any minute. I'm going to run and get dressed before they get here."

"Thank you so much for everything you've done." Jill again stood, this time without stumbling. She walked up to Caroline hugging her tightly. "If it wasn't for you, this wouldn't be happening."

"Ah, the guys did most of the work." Caroline hugged her back before pulling away. "I just ordered them around, which I have to admit, I'm very good at."

"Is Slade here?" Jill asked, a slight blush spreading across her cheeks.

"With the biggest grin on his face." Caroline smiled, then rushed to the door. "Now finish getting more beautiful than you already are while I go change and get the girls ready."

Running to the room next door, Caroline rushed to get dressed, then applied a little makeup and fluffed her hair. Loud knocking from downstairs had her grabbing her high heels before running down the steps to open the door.

Nicole, Tessa, Pam, Lana, and Angelina all stood in the open doorway looking a little confused. "Hey!" Caroline opened the door wider, inviting them in.

Lana stepped inside, her eyes narrowing on Caroline. "What are you doing here?" she whispered, already suspicious.

They all held presents and Caroline suddenly didn't know what to say, her eyes shooting upstairs then back to the ladies. "Ah, you can just set the gifts on the kitchen table."

Nicole looked around with a growing frown. "Are we too early?"

After all the presents were set on the table, they all turned to look at Caroline. "This isn't a bridal shower." Caroline began wringing her hands together. "Jill asked that you all come."

"So if it's not a bridal shower, then what is it?" Tessa asked.

"Don't make me interrogate you, Caroline." Lana narrowed her eyes. "Because I will and you'll blab like you always do."

Caroline cringed, knowing her sister was right, but not this time. "Jill has planned something special for all of you." Emotions threatened to overwhelm Caroline, but she held it back. "Follow me."

"Caroline," Lana warned in her cop voice.

"Please don't question me," Caroline said, but not just to Lana, to all of them. Thankfully, they remained quiet and followed her into a bedroom downstairs. Walking to the closet, Caroline grabbed two white dresses handing one to Angelina and the other to Tessa. She continued to pass out the dresses until they all had one, not looking at any of them in the eye. She was going to see this done. Bending down she grabbed the shoeboxes next, handing one to each of them that had their names on it.

"What is this?" Pam's voice held confusion as she looked at her dress and shoebox.

"Please put the dresses and shoes on. There is makeup on the dresser as well as brushes and hair stuff. As soon as you're dressed, I'll meet you in the kitchen." Caroline walked out and hurriedly shut the door behind her praying they would do what she said. She seriously felt like she was going to have a damn panic attack. Wedding planning was so not her forte. She'd rather be in the classroom with a hundred preschoolers than go through this again.

\*\*\*\*\*\*

Jill stood while her mom laced up her dress. The long mirror Trevor had brought up from her mom and dad's bedroom stood against the wall. Jill couldn't stop staring at herself. She actually looked pretty. Her mom, being a hairdresser, had done her hair and makeup, but it was the dress that kept catching her eyes. It was a white silk sleeveless swoop neck, off-the-shoulder wedding dress that fit tight to the waist and then flared out into flowing lace with no train. It was a simple dress for a simple girl. Looking back at her face, she was happy that her mother was good with makeup. Her dark circles had all but disappeared from under her eyes.

"Okay, turn around and let me see you," her mother said after finishing lacing up the back of the dress. As Jill turned, her mom raised her hand and placed it across her mouth with a gasp.

"What?" Jill put her hand up to her face. "Did I mess something up?"

Her mom laughed, shaking her head. "No. You look stunning."

"I'm not as good at being a girl like Janie." Jill grinned. "I bet she looked beautiful on her wedding day."

A dark look passed over her mother's face. "I haven't talked to your sister in quite some time. Your father refused to let her boyfriend on the property after the day he held the gun on you."

"I'm sorry." Jill touched her mother's arm. "I didn't mean to cause any problems."

"Jill, you didn't cause anything." Her mother frowned. "Chuck was right, and since that day, I've done a lot of thinking and realized how badly I've treated you."

"Hey," Jill said when her mom wouldn't make eye contact with her. "It's my wedding day. Let's not do this. You don't need to explain anything to me. It's the past."

Her mom nodded and then her eyes sprang open. "I almost forgot."

She ran over to the dresser pulling out a small box. "Something old, something new, something borrowed and something blue which will match your hair." She teased.

Jill took the box and opened it. Inside was a pearl choker with white and light blue pearls. "It's absolutely beautiful."

"It's very old." Her mom took it from her and walked around to slip it on Jill. "It has been in my family for I don't even know how long, but it has been passed down from generation to generation to the daughters in the family."

After it was clasped around her neck, Jill turned and walked closer to the mirror. It was perfect and the finishing touch she needed. "It's perfect." Jill grinned, touching it, then looked at her blue tipped hair. "And it does match my hair. Slade likes my hair."

"And why wouldn't he?" her mother replied, her eyes lifting from the choker to Jill. "It's who you are. Now, are you ready?"

Jill took one last glance at herself and nodded. "Yes." But as she headed down the steps, her stomach knotted painfully with nerves. Walking into the kitchen, she stopped and stared, a large smile spreading across her face. "You all look so beautiful."

Everyone stopped talking and turned toward Jill. Suddenly, the kitchen was filled with screams, questions and laughter.

"Oh, my God, Jill." Nicole put both hands on her cheeks staring at her. "You are so beautiful."

Jill went over and carefully hugged each one of them. "Thank you guys so much for everything." She stood back looking at them excitedly. "I know you have questions, but please trust me on this and go with it."

"Everything is ready." Caroline smiled at Jill, then the women. "Follow me please."

She knew everyone was dying to know what was going on, but Jill just smiled at their questioning looks. She watched as each left the kitchen looking gorgeous in their simple white dresses, each unique in their own way. Jill wanted to clap her hands in excitement.

Stepping onto the porch she watched as Caroline matched each woman up with someone. Sloan walked up to Nicole taking her arm gently and walking her toward the woods. Next was Tessa who was matched with Blaze, Pam with Jax, Lana with her own father, and Angelina with Steve.

Jill stood watching the women. She wondered if they had a clue what was going on. It was kind of obvious, but she knew the plan and they didn't. Her smile beamed as her dad hurried toward her.

"You are beautiful." He hugged her gently. "Are you ready?"

"Thanks, Dad." Jill laughed and tried her best not to cry. "I love you."

"I love you, too, Jelly Bean." He hooked her arm into his and followed the line. "Be careful. Your heels might sink in the dirt."

"I'm good." She reached down and lifted her dress, showing her bare feet.

Her dad leaned his head back, releasing a loud laugh. "I taught you well."

Jill smiled with a nod as they continued. They made it to the bend where everyone stopped. Jill and her dad walked past the other couples so Jill could watch everything. Caroline was handing each woman a bouquet of beautiful red roses.

Sloan led Nicole around the bend where Damon was waiting looking handsome in his tux. Sloan stopped, letting go of Nicole as Damon kneeled in front of her. Bowing his head, he thumped his fist against his heart before looking up at her. "Nicole DeMasters, will you do me the honor of renewing our love?"

"Oh, my God," Nicole replied, her voice cracking with emotion. "Yes!" He stood leading her away.

Jill peeked at the rest of the ladies who had positioned themselves so they could see. Every single one of them were staring in wide-eyed shock.

Next, Blaze led Tessa to Jared, who also kneeled repeating the motion of bowing his head, thumping his heart with his fist before looking up. "Tessa Pride, I love you more than my own life. Please say you will be my wife."

Tessa was crying so hard from watching Nicole and Damon, she could hardly say yes. When she nodded enthusiastically, everyone chuckled. Jared slipped a ring on her finger as he stood, leading her away.

Jax led Pam to Duncan who was holding Daniel. Duncan kneeled with Daniel in his arms, still able to pound his chest with his fist, his head bowed. Daniel, who was watching Duncan, repeated his moves making everyone sigh loudly. "My heart, will you make me the happiest man in the world and become my wife as you are already my mate?"

"Yes." Pam smiled, her golden eyes shining as she looked at the two men in her life.

Duncan held out his hand as Daniel's small fist opened up dropping a ring into his hand, which Duncan proceeded to put on her finger. He stood, guiding her away.

Sid walked up next with the biggest grin on his face as Lana and Caroline's father led Lana to him. Kneeling, he bowed his head, pounding his fist over his heart before looking up. "Lana Banana, my sexy cop. Will you please marry me so I can call you mine?"

Lana laughed with a nod. "I'm already yours, Sidilicious." Everyone snickered at the nickname. "But yes, I will marry you."

He grinned proudly as he placed the ring on her finger.

A beaming Steve led a crying Angelina to Adam. Adam kneeled, bowed his head and thumped his heart as the others before him. "My Angel." Adam looked up, his face pale as he stared at

Angelina. "I would be honored for you to be my wife. Will you marry me?"

Angelina put her face in her hands as she nodded, trying to get control of her emotions. Removing her hands, she smiled through her tears. "Yes!" she cried. "I can't believe this." Adam placed the ring on her finger and led her away.

Jill attempted to keep herself together, but was failing miserably. Her father started walking, holding onto her hand to keep her steady. Her eyes looked around as everyone stood up. Some faces she knew, others she didn't, and yet it didn't matter. She looked around and sighed. This was exactly how she had envisioned her wedding when she was a little girl. Her eyes landed on Slade who had stepped forward and waited for her, giving her father the chance to walk his daughter down the aisle, and how sweet was that. She couldn't look away from him. He was so handsome in his tux as he waited for her. His eyes roamed her body before searching her eyes. She always shivered when he gave her *that* look, the look of ownership. Some women would balk at such a look, but she thrived knowing that she was his, because the truth was she did belong to him, heart, body and soul.

Once they reached him, her father gave her a kiss on the cheek then placed her hand in Slade's. "Take care of my girl," Chuck ordered with a fatherly nod before turning and sitting down.

"Yes, sir," Slade answered and never sounded more serious in his life.

Jill stared up in Slade's eyes and everything but him disappeared. The people, their friends, her sickness…it all disappeared for a split second.

"I have never seen anything more beautiful than you." Slade's deep voice rang out through the woods. "I love you now more than I have ever thought possible and I thank you for agreeing to be my mate…my wife."

Jill's head dropped slightly, her eyes closed for a brief second only to open them to make sure this wasn't a dream. It wasn't. Slade was still there staring at her as if she were the most important person in his life.

# CHAPTER 20

The ceremony was quick with each couple saying I do. Jill gazed into Slade's eyes as he and the others began to chant. Backing away, each groom stood in front of their mate as other Warriors lined up at the back of them, all chanting as one. In one motion, the Warriors stopped in unison. All the grooms kneeled on one knee in front of their mates, the rest following again in perfect timing. Their right arm crossed, they placed their fists over their hearts. Heads bowed, chanting in a language that was foreign to Jill. She felt their loyalty without knowing their words. She had never been more touched in her life.

All the Warriors stood, except for the grooms, who remained kneeling with heads bowed to their mates. One by one, each Warrior in attendance stopped in front of each bride stating their name, vowing their loyalty to each. After the last one, each groom stood and walked to their mate.

Jill shivered, her eyes meeting Slade's intense gaze.

"I, Slade Jonathan Buchanan, vow to keep you, Jillian Robin Nichols, safe forever and always." His words were spoken with such conviction tears slipped from Jill's eyes. With everything going on, his words meant so much more.

Jill didn't hear anything other than Slade's words. She only had eyes for him. He took her in his arms placing a kiss on her lips that set her on fire. Too soon, his lips left hers and he smiled down at her.

"I love you, Jillian Buchanan." His voice sent shivers through her body.

"I love you...husband." She laughed and for a moment, everything but that moment was forgotten.

Soon, they were surrounded by loved ones. Everyone talking at once, Jill remained quiet with a glow of happiness on her face as she savored every single second.

"This was supposed to be your day." Nicole walked up to Jill hugging her close. "How did you pull this off?"

Jill's eyes sought out Caroline who was waiting patiently with others to congratulate them. "It was my idea, but Caroline put it all together with the help of the men." Jill held Slade's hand tightly. "And this is *our* day."

After hugging Tessa, Lana, Pam, and Angelina, she let her eyes take in the scene around her. This was *her* clearing, the one she had sat, played and laid dreaming of a simple, but beautiful wedding. Her heart was definitely full. Dusk was falling and the tiny lights in the trees and bushes made it look magical and, in truth, it was magical.

Spotting Trevor, she watched as he held up a finger at her, walked away from the crowd and pointed at their vine, which was decorated with lights. He swung it as if inviting her. Okay, he wasn't inviting her. The ass was daring her. Giving him a narrowed glare, she laughed when he shrugged.

"Jilly!" Seth fought his way through the small crowd surrounding Jill and Slade.

Slade swooped him up before Seth could jump on Jill. His laughter at being caught in midair echoed through the clearing. "Hey there, little man." Slade smiled at the boy. "You don't want to get your sister's pretty dress dirty, do you?"

Seth shook his head, his eyes roaming Jill. "No."

"Look how handsome you are." Jill fixed his little bow tie.

Seth beamed, looking down trying to see his tie. "Mom said I can keep my costume."

"She did?" Jill's eyes opened wide in mock surprise.

"Yep, and I'm going to wear it every day." Seth wiggled to get out of Slade's arms.

Slade set Seth on the ground and they both watched him run off having the time of his life.

"I hope I did everything you asked." Caroline made her way close to Jill and Slade.

"It's absolutely perfect," Jill cried, pulling Caroline into a hug. "Even better than I ever imagined."

"Thank you." Slade also hugged Caroline.

"It was my pleasure. Thank you for letting me be a part of this." Caroline glanced around with a proud smile. "I'm going to grab my helpers and get the tables set up to make room for dancing."

Jill nodded, feeling her excitement build. "That sounds great. Thank you."

"No, thank you." Caroline tossed her a wicked grin. "It's not every day a girl can order handsomely dressed Warriors around." She winked at Jill before walking away.

******

Running around, Caroline made sure everything was perfect. She had spotted Jax and secretly hoped he would ask her to dance. Damn, that man was fine looking in a tux. With one last look at him, she spun and ran into her mom and dad.

"Slow down, honey." Her dad caught and steadied her. "We've been trying to catch up with you all night."

Caroline held onto her dad with a laugh. "I'm sorry." She kissed his cheek, then her mom's. "This has been the craziest experience I've ever had."

"You've done a beautiful job." Her mother looked around with tears in her eyes. "I am so proud of my two girls."

"Thanks, Mom." Caroline glanced at her younger sister, Jamie. "So what do you think?"

"Who is that?" Jamie answered her question with a question.

Caroline's gaze followed Jamie's landing on Hunter. "Oh, no you don't." Caroline stepped in Jamie's line of vision. "He's way too old for you."

"Yeah, but he's hot." Jamie grinned, trying to look around Caroline.

"Come on, Jamie." Her mom dragged Jamie in the opposite direction.

"And I thought you and Lana were a handful." Her father sighed. "How's the house coming along?"

Caroline had waited for the question and there it was. She knew her dad was only being a dad so she smiled. "It's going," she answered, then laughed at his downfallen expression. "It's going well, Dad. Now stop worrying."

"I'm your father. I worry," he replied. "You keeping your doors locked and your gun near you?"

The mention of door locks sent her mind swirling with thoughts of Jax, but she pushed them back. "Yes, sir."

He narrowed his eyes at her, working his human lie detector on her. She must have passed, because his face softened. "Okay, I'll let you be and get back to what you were doing." He squeezed her hand. "I'll talk to you later. Love you."

"Love you, too, Dad," she said to his retreating back. Caroline went back to making sure everything was running smoothly. A line was forming where the caterers were set up and the food smelled delicious. She realized she hadn't eaten anything since that morning and her stomach growled loudly in agreement.

Greeting a few people, she made her way to the food, but spotted Steve near the cake. "Don't you dare," she scolded, watching as he discreetly lifted a finger toward the beautiful three-tiered cake.

"I know." Steve spun around, his eyes wide with guilt. "It's a sickness. I crave icing so badly, have since I was little and can't keep from doing one swipe of the finger so I can taste it."

Caroline really tried not to smile at his confession. In truth, she was the exact same way and wanted more than anything to do just that. "Step away from the cake, Steve." She used the cop voice she had heard Lana use.

Steve raised his hands in the air, stepping away from the cake, then smiled before turning toward the food table.

Caroline laughed, but her eyes went to the cake, her fingers itching to take a swipe. "Don't do it." She told herself, forcing her feet to move away.

"So what are you doing after this eating thing?" Hunter asked one of the pretty caterers, holding up the line.

Caroline knew the poor girl was a goner when she stared at Hunter in awed fascination. Stepping up beside Hunter, Caroline grabbed a plate. She knew she was cutting, but she had the job of saving this poor girl from the big bad wolf. "Hey."

Hunter growled at his flirting being interrupted. "Hey."

Caroline placed three meatballs on her plate as she nodded toward the female bartender across the clearing. "She wanted me to let you know she's off duty in a couple of hours and to meet her on the trail."

Hunter fully turned to Caroline, a 'that was so not cool' expression on his face. "Really."

Caroline knew he wasn't asking a question, but she pretended he had. "Yeah, really." She nodded with wide-eyed innocence.

They both glanced at the pretty caterer whose furious glare indicated she was no longer interested. Hunter huffed, moving down the line and Caroline followed, putting a few more tasty treats on her plate. When they were away from the table, Hunter gave her a hurt look.

"That was mean." He plopped a meatball in his mouth.

"You were holding up the line and that girl was too innocent for you." Caroline raised her eyebrow at him.

Hunter chewed thoughtfully for a minute before glancing at the bartender. "So did you really talk to the bartender?"

"Seriously, Hunter?!" Caroline's head snapped back as she walked away from him. "You are too much."

"That's what they all say," Hunter called after her, plopping another meatball in his mouth, a wicked grin spreading across his face.

Shaking her head, Caroline swiped a beer from the bartender then headed for one of the tables further back in the clearing. Sitting down, she toed off her high heels with a relieved sigh of pleasure. As she ate, she watched everyone and was pleased to see no problems. Sid and Lana were on the dance floor slow dancing. She could practically feel the heat from where she was sitting. They made a beautiful couple. They all made beautiful couples. Her eyes landed on Blaze who was talking with a pretty red head. Caroline really didn't know Katrina very well, but she seemed sweet.

Taking a long swig of beer, Caroline leaned back in her chair and closed her eyes for a few seconds, wiggling her bare toes in the cool grass. She was wiped out.

"Care to dance?"

Caroline knew by the voice it wasn't the man she really wanted to dance with, but she smiled and opened her eyes. "So the great and powerful Sloan dances?"

"I've been known to tear up a dance floor or two." He grinned, holding out his hand.

She took another drink of beer before letting him pull her from the chair. "Oh, I bet you have."

******

Jax stood in the shadows watching Sloan approach Caroline and then lead her out to dance. The low growl building in his chest escaped when Sloan pulled her close saying something that made Caroline laugh.

"I think it would be really bad for you to kill your boss." Hunter had appeared at his side, a beer in one hand and a shot glass in the other. "Here, you need this more than me."

Looking down at the shot, Jax grabbed it and downed it in a second flat. "Thanks."

"Welcome." Hunter gave a short nod. "Yeah, your sweet little Caroline pretty much ruined my night."

Jax looked away from Caroline for a split second. "How so?"

Hunter told Jax what Caroline had done, all the while a small grin of respect curved his lips. "So now all the pretty ladies here think I'm a player."

"Aren't you?" Jax raised an eyebrow.

"Ah, yeah." Hunter snorted. "But it was a secret until your girl blabbed."

"Caroline is not my girl." Jax wished he had another shot of whiskey.

"They have a history?" Hunter pointed his beer toward Sloan and Caroline.

"No," he answered, but then realized he wasn't really sure.

"Then you better make a move my friend, before they do." Hunter gave him a parting look before walking off.

"You're still on the job," Jax called out after him. "You need to worry about that instead of playing matchmaker."

Hunter just threw up his hand in a wave, indicating he heard him loud and clear.

"Asshole," Jax grumbled, his eyes focused back on Caroline who was walking back to her table, alone. Jax headed her way. He'd be damned if he left without dancing with her at least once.

As soon as he made his way to her, she bent to pick up her shoes. His eyes automatically went to her ass which was cupped beautifully in her pale blue summer dress that fit her body perfectly. She straightened without the shoes and turned around, a small smile blooming across her lips.

"Hi." She smoothed her dress, her eyes never leaving his.

"You look beautiful." Jax's voice was deep with a rough edge.

"Awe, thank you." She gave him a once over. "And you are very handsome in a tux, Jax Wheeler."

Jax cursed himself for being so awkward, his hand fidgeting in the pocket of his slacks as he stared at her. "Dance with me."

"I thought you'd never ask." Caroline's voice turned husky, making his desire for her soar.

Instead of taking her where others were slow dancing, he pulled her in his arms and danced her into the shadows. Her softness against his hardness was almost more than he could stand. Sloan's scent still lingered on her, his alpha side reared its ugly head. "You and Sloan have a thing going?" he asked a little more harshly than he intended.

"Sloan?" Caroline moved her head off his chest to stare up at him. "No. I mean he's very handsome, but..."

Anger consumed him. "It's a yes or no question, Caroline."

"Oh, then no." Caroline touched the corner of his mouth gently. "You really shouldn't frown so much, Jax."

"Then don't tell me you find other men handsome," Jax replied, surprised the words came out of his mouth. What the fuck was wrong with him? He knew exactly what was wrong with him and he was holding her in his arms.

# CHAPTER 21

Jill finally found a minute to sit down and glared at the pack of crackers sitting on the table. With a huff she grabbed one while her eyes roamed. Spotting Slade talking to Jax and Caroline, she looked back at her cracker.

"Let me have one of those." Adam sat down grabbing a cracker and glared at it.

"To us." Jill held up her cracker for a toast.

Adam chuckled, tapping her cracker with his. "To us."

They both took a bite and chewed. "Mmmmm." Jill tried to sound like the cracker was the best thing she'd ever eaten, but her face of disgust said otherwise.

"It tastes like ass," Adam grumbled, tossing the cracker down on the table.

"Don't know what ass tastes like, but thanks for making the only food I can eat less appetizing." Jill threw the cracker aside.

"Sorry," Adam said with a sheepish grin. "Thanks, Jill. What you've done means so much to all of us."

"Don't thank me, Adam." Jill sighed with a happy smile. "It's what I wanted to do. This is my family and sharing this with you all has been awesome."

Adam nodded, but kept silent.

"Can I ask you a personal question?" This was going to be awkward as hell, but she needed to know before tonight.

"You can ask me anything, Jill. You know that." Adam closed his eyes leaning his head back. "Shoot."

"Did Slade tell you not to…you know…" Jill cringed in embarrassment. "…with Angelina tonight?"

Adam opened one eye to peek over at her. "Have sex?"

Jill only nodded, knowing her face flushed bright red.

"Hell no." Adam shut his eye. "And if he did, I'd laugh in his face and tell him to go…you know what…himself."

"So you and Angelina have been—"

"Yes, Jill," Adam interrupted her. "Now, how about we stop taking about this. I didn't know when you said personal question it meant *that*."

"What did you think I meant?" Jill asked, curling her bare toes in the cool grass, enjoying the feel.

"I don't know." Adam sighed. "Something like…have I been having a hard time pissing since I've been sick." Again he peeked at her with one eye.

"Oh." Jill frowned. "Have you?"

Adam sat up. "Yeah, but I think I'm dehydrated."

"You need to tell Slade," Jill demanded.

"I will after tonight," Adam promised then chuckled. "We sure get ourselves in some messes, don't we? Here we are on our wedding night talking about having a hard time pissing."

Jill slapped her hand over her mouth and soon they were laughing so hard they couldn't breathe. At the same time, they took deep breaths through their noses and sighed.

"Damn, that food smells so fucking good." Adam took one more deep breath.

"I know," Jill agreed, wanting to pinch her nose closed so she couldn't smell it anymore. "Are you scared, Adam?"

Adam wouldn't meet her gaze; instead, he stood and kissed her on top of the head before walking away.

With her stomach cramping painfully, Jill stood, ignoring it the best she could. Strong arms wrapped around her from behind.

"You ready, Mrs. Buchanan?" Slade's voice whispered in her ear.

"Ready for what?" She leaned into him, savoring his strength and loving her new name.

"You're not the only one with surprises." Slade kissed the side of her neck. "Let's say our goodbyes."

Jill nodded in agreement, excitement mixing with the pain in her stomach.

******

After their goodbyes, Slade picked her up carrying her up the trail toward the house. Her bare feet stuck out from her dress.

"You forgot your shoes." Slade stopped, ready to turn around.

"No, I didn't." Jill wiggled her toes. "I didn't wear any."

"At all?" Slade grinned.

"Nope." Jill kissed his cheek. "You married a true country girl, Slade Buchanan."

"Have fun you two." Caroline met them on the path coming from the house. "Everything is set," she told Slade.

"Thank you, Caroline." Slade moved to the side letting her pass.

"What's going on?" Jill frowned at both of them. When they remained silent, Jill knew she wasn't going to get any answers. "Okay, well, leave everything, Caroline. You've done enough and I'll be back to clean up."

"I've got this, Jill," Caroline told her. "Now get her out of here, Slade."

"Caroline." Jill huffed. "I mean it."

All Jill heard from Caroline was a laugh. Frowning, she looked up the path and sitting in her parents' driveway was a sleek black limo, and Slade was heading right for it.

"That's for us?" Jill asked in awe. She'd never ridden in a limo before.

Slade set her down gently as the driver opened the door. "It's for you."

Looking at the driver before getting in, Jill thanked him. Scooting across the seat, her eyes were round as saucers. "It's beautiful." She took everything in.

"You're beautiful," Slade replied, watching her.

"I've never been in a limo before, can ya tell?" She laughed at herself climbing onto Slade's lap, wrapping her arms around his neck.

"If this is the way you show your appreciation, I'll buy you one." Slade kissed her softly. "What color would you like?"

"Blue," Jill answered automatically. "I want a blue limo."

"Blue to match your hair." Slade touched her face with a soft caress.

"You know me so well," Jill teased, pressing her face into his hand.

"I'm learning more and more about you every single day." Slade's eyes roamed her face.

"That's a scary thought." Jill cringed.

"No, it's fascinating." He took her mouth in a gentle kiss that quickly turned into something more intense.

*Finally!* Jill shouted silently in her mind, but as soon as things were getting hot and she was on the verge of losing her mind in a good way, Slade pulled away from her. "No!" This time the word came out of her mouth and loudly.

Slade chuckled. "Unless you want the driver to get a peek at the action, we need to slow it down."

Regaining her wits, which took a few minutes, Jill realized they had stopped. Slade tapped on the window, the door opened right away. Slade slid out first, then held his hand out to help Jill. She turned to find a cute little cabin surrounded by trees.

"I figured you wouldn't want to spend your wedding night at the compound." Slade led her around the limo and then tipped the driver who had set two small suitcases on the porch.

"It's perfect, Slade." Jill beamed. "It's almost like the one I showed you a while ago, that I loved."

Slade smiled, took a key out of his pocket and opened the door. Carefully picking her up, he carried her into the cabin and set her down.

Jill stood in the middle of the room just taking everything in. The fireplace was a gorgeous stone and already had a fire crackling. She walked slowly, peeking into another room and gasped. The kitchen was huge and rustic, just like the cabin itself.

"Sid would kill for this kitchen." Jill laughed, opening doors and soaking up the beauty of the place. Continuing her exploration, she headed upstairs. "It has two nice size bedrooms. The cabin doesn't look this big on the outside."

"Did you look out back?" Slade called from downstairs.

Jill came back down the steps, excitement shining from her eyes. She opened the double doors, walked out onto a patio and clapped in delight. "A pool!" Jill spun around, laughing. "Please tell me we can go swimming."

"We can do whatever you want," Slade said, without realizing the implication of his words, but Jill heard him loud and clear. "So do you really like it?"

"I absolutely love it, Slade." Jill wrapped her arms around herself, feeling like the luckiest woman in the world. "How long are we staying?"

"For as long as you want." Slade pulled her to him putting his chin on top of her head. "Because I bought it for you."

"Excuse me?" Jill pulled away, her nails clawing into his arms. "What did you say?"

"It's ours, Jill." Slade chuckled at her open-mouth gape.

"You...you bought me a house?" she said. He nodded, yet she still didn't believe it.

"I love you." Slade tilted her chin up. "I would buy you the world if I could."

"No." She shook her head, her eyes still wide with shock. "A house is good, but it's too much."

"Be prepared to be spoiled, Mrs. Buchanan." Slade picked her up so he had easy access to her mouth. "Because I plan on doing much more of it."

"I don't need to be spoiled, but I do need to be loved, by you." Jill kissed him with all the passion she had inside her. She knew he knew exactly what she wanted, what she needed. "Please, Slade."

"Jill." His tone changed from sexy Slade to Dr. Buchanan.

"You never told Adam he couldn't have sex with Angelina." Jill dropped her bombshell on him.

"You're not Adam," Slade replied, letting her go when she wiggled.

"No, I'm not." Jill backed away, reaching behind her to pull the string to unlace her dress, and wouldn't you know it, her mother had knotted it. So much for stripping with a sexy flare. Instead, she pushed down her off-the-shoulder sleeves until she bared her breasts, which his darkening eyes went straight to. Thankfully, the lace had loosened over the hours of wearing the dress and she was able to shimmy her way out of it.

Standing before Slade in only a lacey white thong, Jill gave him her sexiest smile. "Tell me no now, Slade." And God, she prayed he didn't tell her no, because that would devastate her as well as being the most embarrassing moment of her life.

Slade adjusted his crotch as he continued to stare at her. Her eyes dropped to watch him and smiled at the huge bulge in his tux slacks. She wished she had high heels on, but she had to go with what she had. Turning around, on purpose of course, she bent and picked up her dress giving him the best view of her ass. Walking toward the steps with her wedding dress in her arms, she stopped and looked over her shoulder.

"I'll be upstairs, Slade." She purposely ran her eyes over his body, stopping at the bulge for a second longer. "I'm not above begging or playing dirty." She tossed him a sexy grin; at least, she hoped it was sexy. She was just now learning the art of being sexy. Climbing the steps, she prayed to God she wouldn't trip and that her climb showed him all her assets that she was overly exerting to draw his attention. Taking a peek, she grinned when his eyes were exactly where she wanted them.

Jill walked into the biggest bedroom, a huge grin on her face. Well, even if he didn't ravish her, he'd be as uncomfortable as she had been. Jill jumped when the door slammed behind her.

"You don't play fair." Slade ripped off his shirt, buttons flying everywhere.

"Oh, isn't that rented?" Jill watched the buttons bounce along the floor.

"I don't give a fuck about the shirt." He growled as he stalked toward her, his eyes burning black.

Okay, maybe, just maybe she pushed him too far.

"Take it off," he demanded. When she didn't react fast enough, he reached out and with expert ease, he ripped her lace thong off her body. She hissed in pleasure as he slid it between her legs, tossing it on the floor.

Raising her hands eagerly to his belt buckle, he grasped her hands, holding them together with one hand as he himself undid his buckle and completely stripped away the rest of his clothes.

"This will be on my terms, Jillian." Slade's voice was rough. "You are to do nothing, but enjoy me as I worship every part of your body. I want no argument whatsoever from you. Is that understood?"

Was he crazy? What woman in her right mind would argue with those terms? All she could do was nod her agreement.

Picking her up, he gently laid her on the bed, but still held her hands above her head. He did just as he promised, worshipped every part of her body, driving her insane with need. If the serum sickness didn't kill her, this certainly would.

"Please, Slade." Jill panted, needing to find release, and soon. It had been too long.

Slade let go of her hands. "Do not move them," he ordered as he climbed between her legs and lifted her knees from the bed.

She loved the dominant part of him that came out in the bedroom. Even though sometimes it drove her absolutely crazy, she loved it. Their eyes met as he slowly slid into her. She started to rise to meet his thrust, but he growled down at her.

"Do not move." He leaned down and kissed her as he began to pump hard and fast, using his own strength to bring her up to meet his thrusts.

She realized what he was doing. Not only was he taking care of her needs, he was making sure she used no energy by doing all the work himself. She had never loved him more than she did at that moment. He loved her *that* much.

He pulled his mouth away and she was happy to let him go because she could watch him as he loved her. The snarl on his face was sexy because she knew he was fighting back his own release until she found hers. He looked down to watch as their bodies met in a fast tempo and when he raised his eyes to hers, they were black as midnight, rimmed with red as his sharp fangs protruded, giving him a wild untamed look.

Jill's body burst into what felt like flames. It was the strongest orgasm she had ever had. It shook her to the core, lasting for what seemed like hours. Slade's body trembled for just as long. Using his arms to keep his body weight off her, he leaned down and kissed her, careful not to slice her with his fangs.

"Are you okay?" Slade's voice was hoarse.

"You're not allowed to ask me that anymore." Jill touched his cheek. "But yes, I'm more than okay. I'm fantastic."

"I love you." Slade's voice actually cracked and for the first time, Jill saw the fear he couldn't hide shimmering in his eyes. Pulling him to her, she held him tight.

"I love you more," she whispered before closing her eyes. It was time to put her next plan into motion.

# CHAPTER 22

"I can't believe Duncan turned himself in," Steve grumbled from the driver's seat. "And Sloan let him. Hell, Sloan took him."

Jill sat in the passenger seat feeling numb at the news when she and Slade had returned to the compound. Slade had known it was going to happen and purposely kept it from her, but then again, what could she have done? Nothing, that was what. Absolutely nothing.

But that was about to change. She understood that the Warriors' hands were tied, but she was a new Warrior and not high up. She was going to do this and no one, other than herself, could get in trouble. She ensured that no one else knew, except for Steve, but Steve was just her driver.

"They have a different sense of duty than we do, Steve," Jill replied, sitting up straighter as they hit downtown Cincinnati.

"Yeah, well, I would never turn you or Adam in, that's for damn sure." Steve clicked on his blinker. "Even though every Warrior in there scares the shit out of me, I wouldn't turn you in."

"A lot of things scare the shit out of you, Steve," Jill mumbled, trying to read street signs.

"Keeps my bowels in tip-top shape," Steve replied, so serious that Jill's head snapped toward him. "Well, it does."

She didn't know how in the hell he did it, but in any dire situation, Steve could say something so off the wall that she couldn't help but laugh and laugh she did, so much so she started to dry heave. "Shit, Steve, you're going to kill me."

"I do what I can, babe... I do what I can." Steve got into the furthest left lane turning on his hazards. "I think that's it."

"I don't know." Jill moved closer to the windshield to see. "Are you sure?"

The van in front of them moved and what it revealed made both

Steve and Jill glance at each other. News trucks and reporters lined the street. Jill looked up at the building they were in front of. In big elaborate lettering, it said City Hall.

"Holy shit on a stick." Steve had parked on the street in a spot someone had just pulled out of.

"I can't do this." Jill's insides literally shook as she watched all the reporters standing around. "What in the hell did you tell them?"

"You told me to get the media here and that's what I did. I told them there was a government cover-up that was going to be exposed." Steve grinned, proud of his achievement.

"Seriously, I don't think I can do this." Jill hated to admit that, but it was true.

"Yes, you can." Steve slammed his hand on the dashboard. "You are woman. Let them hear you roar."

"I so want to kill you right now." Jill sneered at him. "I hate that fucking song."

"What in the hell are you waiting for?" Hunter slammed his hands on the top of the car while sticking his face through the open window.

Jill jumped, screaming. "What are you doing here?" When she saw Adam standing behind Hunter, Jill cursed. "Dammit, Steve."

"I'm sorry, but I felt we needed some backup." Steve gave his empty apology. He didn't look apologetic in the least. "I tried to get her pumped up with that 'I Am Woman, Hear Me Roar' song, but she's just not feeling it."

Struggling with the door, she pushed her way out before she actually killed Steve. Standing, she swayed, but Hunter steadied her.

"Let's just calm down." Hunter forced her to look at him with a light shake. "Jill, this was your plan. Do you believe in what you set out to do here?"

"Of course I do." Jill nodded, making her dizzy so she stopped.

"Then let's go do it." Hunter gave her a wink. "We're behind you. You won't be alone."

Jill took a deep breath. "If he sings that fucking song one more time." Jill knew she was stalling, but she couldn't help it.

"I'll kill him myself," Hunter assured her without cracking a grin.

"Okay." Jill almost nodded, but stopped. "Okay! Let's do this."

Steve, Hunter, and Adam surrounded Jill as they walked up the steps to City Hall. Jill tried to keep her eyes straight ahead, but she did see Steve giving reporters nods, and soon they had a crowd following them.

"I think I'm going to get sick," Jill whispered, holding onto Adam's hand.

"What the fuck are you going to throw up?" Adam whispered back. "You been holding out on me and found something better than crackers?"

Jill choked out a laugh, then leaned in toward Adam. "I'm having a hard time pissing," she admitted with a whisper not knowing why she shared that with him, but just felt the need to do so.

"Welcome to the club." Adam opened the door allowing Jill to go in first. "After this is over, we can compare symptoms."

"Deal." Jill's smile faded as they were met with a metal detector. She didn't bring her weapon and hoped the guys didn't either or she would be going in there alone. Jill started to go through, but the officer running it stopped her.

"What business do you have here?" The officer's tone was nasty.

"I'm here for the—" Jill started, but was interrupted.

"Step to the side and let these people pass," the officer ordered.

Jill did as she was told. Tension rolled off Adam and Hunter who flanked her. Steve's face was even pinched in a very pissed-off sneer.

Getting a little angry herself, she looked at the reporters and cameramen before trying to walk through again. This time, the officer stepped from behind the screening counter and started to reach for her.

"I'm going to put this as politely as I can and believe me that is not easy for me to do especially when I'm staring into the face of ignorance." Hunter stepped in front of Jill, blocking the officer. "What you are doing is against the law. If she passes through the metal detector without incident, she can legally walk into this building as a US citizen. You are profiling her because she is a half-breed."

"I asked her a question." The officer didn't look too sure of himself.

"Which has no merit," Hunter replied before looking at a pretty reporter with a wink. "Isn't that right? You rolling on this?"

"As a matter of fact, I am." The reporter smiled back at Hunter, then to the officer she held out the mic. "Would you like to explain your reasoning on questioning this young lady when not questioning others?"

The officer gave the reporter and Hunter a dark glare before going back behind the screening table. "Go ahead," the officer snapped.

Jill gave the woman reporter a nod of thanks before walking through the metal detector then waited as Hunter, Adam, and lastly Steve who stared wide-eyed at the officer showing his golden vampire eyes as he passed.

"Maybe you should do the talking." Jill glanced at Hunter.

"Nah, I just used up all my nice," he replied, coming to a stop and looking around. "I'll end up shooting off at the mouth and all will be lost."

"I think that's the room you're looking for." The reporter pointed to a room people were filing into.

"Thank you." Jill smiled as she made her way inside. They found a place to sit near the front and waited. Six men and three women sat on a podium that stretched across the room. One man was talking, but Jill wasn't listening; instead, she focused on what she needed to say and hoped with everything she had she didn't screw this up. She started to turn to see how much media was in the room, but Hunter stopped her.

"Don't," Hunter whispered. "No one other than you and those nine people up there are in this room. Fight, Jill. You're not only speaking for yourself, you're speaking for a whole race."

"We're going to open up now for citizens to express concerns," one man said, drawing Jill's attention.

"You're on." Hunter gave her an encouraging nod.

Steve and Adam touched her as she passed in encouragement. As soon as Jill stood and started toward the podium, a man stood also heading that way.

"Hey, dude," Hunter called out. "Ladies first."

The man, embarrassed, nodded and sat down. A few people snickered.

Jill walked to the podium staring at the microphone. "My name is Jillian Bucha..."

"You need to speak up." One of the men on the council said, looking irritated to have to even say anything.

Her eyes searched each and every one of them and only two, maybe showed any interest in what she had to say and that set her soul on fire adding fuel to her growing anger.

"My name is Jillian Buchanan." Her voice was strong and clear this time.

"I take it you are the reason for all the media here today." Another man who sat on a platform higher than her looked down his narrowed nose.

"Yes." Jill nodded, knowing they were only seeing her mismatched eyes. "I most certainly am and I'm glad I made that call because just getting into this building proved difficult. Only with the help of a reporter was I allowed to walk inside."

"State your business." Another man looked at his watch, not even at her.

"There is only one thing that sets me apart from you," Jill began, taking time to look at each council member. "I love like you. I breathe like you. I even have a heartbeat like you, but the thing that sets me apart from you is I'm a half-breed who has been sentenced to death. As you sit on your platform playing God, I, along with hundreds more are slowly starving to death."

Murmurs from the crowd echoed throughout the room, but Jill wasn't finished.

"By no choice of my own I was given a manmade serum to turn me into a half-breed. The serum is making us sick. The only way to save us is to change us, but a new law you proposed and had passed prohibits any half-breed to be changed. I refuse to let my husband, Dr. Slade Buchanan, change me because of this law. He would lose his VC Warrior status, be jailed, and lose his medical license." Jill's throat swelled with emotion preventing her from saying anything for a second. Jill swayed, black spots dotted across her vision. Swallowing hard, she cleared her throat. "You have already jailed a highly regarded VC Warrior for changing his loved one, I'll be damned if you jail another."

Jill watched as one council member leaned over whispering something to another.

"I am standing before you today to fight for my life. I deserve to live whether I'm human or vampire." This time tears filled her eyes. Her body was weak and the room swayed, but she kept a death grip on the podium because she was not going down until she finished. "This happening to me means it can happen to one of your loved ones, even yourselves."

"Mrs. Buchanan, you need to realize we have to have some kind of regulation," a stuffy older gentleman who eyed her with disdain said into his little microphone.

"Why?" Jill asked, now leaning against the podium. Something was wrong and she was fighting to stay on her feet. Her breathing felt funny and her vision kept bouncing from clear to blurry. When the man didn't answer, Jill's anger skyrocketed. "It's a simple question."

"No, it's not," he replied. "We can't have vampires running around changing people…"

Jill shook her head. "I see that you have no clue what the hell you're talking about." Moving her face away from the microphone, Jill tried to take a couple deep breaths. When Hunter started to come to her, she waved him away, turning back to the microphone. "If by regulation you mean jailing a VC Warrior for saving his wife's life then this council is a lost cause."

"Insubordination will not be tolerated." The old council member's jowls bobbled with anger.

Jill slammed her hand down hard on the podium. "I am fighting for my life as well as the lives of others and you want to talk about insubordination? I speak the truth. What you're doing is a crime. I am a VC Warrior and I swore an oath to protect…protect you…all of you in this room. You are people of power, who can easily do what's right." Jill looked down at her hand which was cramping and clawing, the pain excruciating. "But you refuse to do so because of your fear, and because of your fear, innocent people are suffering."

"Yes, we along with many other councils proposed this law, but you have to understand Mrs. Buchanan the crime rate with your kind is…"

Jill interrupted the old man who sat in judgment of her. "So you decide to see us die when you know the cure." She shook her head as if trying to understand their reasoning. "Not to mention jailing a VC Warrior who upholds the law."

"It is a travesty, but…"

"No!" Jill pointed right at him as she interrupted once again. "For you to have any power over people's lives is a travesty."

Knowing that talking to these people was a waste of time, Jill turned toward the media directly behind her. "I was human, I am still half human. I have the right to live as does hundreds, maybe thousands more who are dying like me. Desperation is going to set in and this law is going to be broken…has been broken, but not by evil. This law is going to be broken by people who are just trying to save their loved ones. Don't let this happen. Fight because it can be yourself or a loved one you're fighting to save next."

A loud roaring echoed in her ears. Her sight dimmed. Dammit she wasn't finished, but knew she couldn't go on. She wanted Slade.

"Mrs. Buchanan, are you okay?" The woman reporter who was closet to her asked.

"No, I'm not," Jill replied, a tear slipping down her cheek.

"Jill?" Adam, Hunter and Steve surrounded her.

"Get me out of here." She whispered, fear filling her soul. "I want Slade."

Hunter and Adam grabbed her. People moved quickly out of the way as they passed, every news camera on her. Once outside on the steps, they were surrounded by more media as well as half-breeds and vampires who must have been watching the news and came in support.

"Let us through." Steve fought to clear a path.

Jill collapsed on the steps. Adam was too weak to do anything. Hunter tried to carry Jill and fight his way through the crowd with Steve. Jill watched it all happen through a dimmed haze of death and knew it was too late for her and she was terrified. She wasn't ready to die.

Hunter laid her down, staring at her with fear and fury, people pushing at him, but he shielded her body with his. One hard push had him falling on top of her. With a roar, he threw his head back. His body rippled as he changed on the steps of City Hall and stood over Jill snapping at anyone who came near. She could hear Steve screaming to someone and felt Adam's hand on her hair.

"I'm so sorry, Jill." Adam's voice shook with tears.

She tried to move her mouth to talk, but nothing would come out. Her heart slowed, her body dimming like a burned-out candle. Her last thought as her eyes closed was of Slade, and in the distance, she heard the cry of a wolf.

******

Slade stood in front of the television in Sloan's office, his eyes glued to Jill who stood fighting for not only herself, but others. He watched as she swayed and held onto the podium, alarms going off in his brain.

"How far is City Hall from here?" Slade frowned when he watched Jill squint her eyes. "How fucking far?"

"About ten minutes with traffic." Sid took his eyes off the screen for a split second.

"Get me out of here." Jill's voice filled the room as they all watched her sway again. "I want Slade."

Slade was the first out the door with everyone following. Within seconds, motorcycles flew out of the parking lot. Sid led the way zooming in and out of traffic. Brake lights for as far as you could see stretched out in front of them. Jared passed them waving his arm. Slade revved his bike and followed up an embankment and out of danger from the cars.

He had to get to her in time. He saw the signs of her body shutting down. She seemed okay when he left this morning, but he knew how fast organs could fail. "Fuck!" Urgency made Slade crazy with fear. "Come on!"

Sid pointed and Slade saw tons of people, cops and ambulances. Slade rode his bike up on the sidewalk, hitting the steps of City Hall before laying the bike down safely away from citizens. His feet didn't miss a beat as he ran knocking people out of the way and then there she was with Steve and Adam trying to guard her. Hunter in wolf form was poised over her growling at anyone who dared to come near.

Sliding to his knees, he reached for her, bringing her to him. "Jill?" He checked her pulse and barely felt it beat against his fingers. "How long has she been like this?"

"About five minutes." Adam's voice was weak, but anger fractured every word.

"I'm here, Jill. Hang on for me." Slade moved his ear to her chest and counted her heartbeats. They were too slow. She wasn't going to make it. "God dammit!" Slade's bellow rang out, making people take a step back. Warriors started showing up and circled Slade and Jill, keeping prying eyes away.

He felt a hand on his shoulder. "Do it." Sloan's voice registered in his mind.

Not that he needed permission, but Jesus, he could still lose her. Slade Buchanan was terrified and broken. He looked down at Jill's pale face to see red teardrops splattering her skin. His fangs elongated as he tilted her neck. He heard the chant of courage coming from the Warriors who stood to protect him as he tried to save the only person who ever mattered to him and the one he loved more than his own life.

# CHAPTER 23

Slade waited as patiently as he could as they processed his paperwork at the jail. Duncan, from what he understood, had been released hours earlier. Jill had done it. She had gotten the law changed and he was so fucking proud of her he could burst.

Because of all the media attention, he had been allowed to stay with Jill until she fully recovered. The City Council members wanted no more bad press. Like they could have stopped him from staying with her. His own death would have been the only thing that kept him from her side. Also Sloan threatening to pull every VC Warrior under him out of the city had made a big impact on allowing Slade to be able to turn himself in at a later date.

It took only two days for Jill to be up on her feet. She hadn't experienced the shock Pam had and for each individual it was different. Some turned fast and others could take weeks while a few didn't make it at all. His Jillian was a strong woman.

Jill had been furious when Slade informed her he was turning himself in. She had to promise not to get a posse together to break him out of jail. She also promised to continue her fight to get the laws changed, which she did with a passion that made him proud.

Adam was also turned a couple of days after Jill, which Sloan took care of. He was ready to turn himself in when he got the call that the law had been changed so lives could be saved. It seemed Jill's plea to the public through media was heard loud and clear across the country.

Finally, a police officer handed him all the stuff he came to jail with. "Thanks." Slade grabbed it all then headed out the door at a run and hit a brick wall. "What the hell?" Slade picked himself off the ground.

"Hope that hurt." Jill stood there with her hands outstretched.

Slade laughed, then tried to move toward her, but she stopped him. "I'm really angry with you." The sun hit Jill's matching golden eyes making them glow. "I told you not to change me."

"Didn't we already have this fight?" Slade couldn't get enough of looking at her.

"Yes, but I was too weak yet to slam you on your ass." Jill frowned. "You did a week in jail and could have lost your medical license."

Dropping what was in his hands, he raised his palm using his power to pull her toward him. "And this is the thanks I get?" Once she was close enough, he swooped her into his arms. "I would die for you, Jillian."

Jill clutched onto him so tight it hurt. "And I would die for you," she said against his chest. "Sloan wouldn't let me come to see you."

"That's because I told him not to." Slade tilted her face to his. "You needed to get your strength back and had no business coming to the jail."

"I tried to sneak, but he had everyone watching me." Jill grumbled making him smile.

Slade buried his face in her hair. "I almost lost you, Jill."

"Yes, you did." Jill touched his face with her hand. "I was just trying to—"

"Save everyone but yourself." Slade finished for her. He bent down kissing her softly, but when she deepened the kiss, he moaned and pulled away. "Let's get the hell out of here. We have some making up to do."

"And I'm thirsty." Jill laid her head against his side as they walked to the car.

"I told Sloan to have you feed from someone." He frowned as he opened the car door for her.

Jill reached up and wrapped her arms around him, kissing him once again deeply. "I refused to feed from anyone but you. Sloan threatened me, punctured his arm and well, I was so thirsty, I couldn't help it and I definitely didn't like it. I don't ever want to feed from anyone other than you again."

Slade forced his anger down. If she had to feed from anyone but himself, he'd rather it be Sloan Murphy, but he still didn't like it. "You needed to feed and couldn't wait a week for me."

"I know, but don't do that to me again." Jill punched him in the stomach.

"Thank you for fighting." Slade brushed some hair out of her beautiful eyes.

"Thank you for giving me something to fight for," she whispered against his lips.

******

Caroline was busy trying to catch up. She hadn't done anything with her house during the marathon wedding, and school would be starting soon. She had to make this place livable. She was tired of sleeping on the floor. She had tried to get another roofer out for another quote, but so far with no luck.

A large truck lumbered down the hole-riddled driveway. Caroline looked out the window before opening the door.

As soon as she walked out the door, he jumped down from his truck. "I'm sorry, but I think you have the wrong address."

"Caroline Fitzpatrick?" he called out, looking up from paperwork.

"Yes." Caroline nodded, placing her hands on her hips.

"Nope, got the right address." He tossed the clipboard back inside the cab of his truck. "Now, where do you want me to put all this stuff?"

"Listen, I didn't order anything." Caroline walked closer. "What is it?"

Three motorcycles came barreling down the driveway. Jax pulled next to the truck and got off his bike. "Sorry, I wanted to be here before the truck pulled in."

"You know about this?" Caroline walked closer, still confused as to what was going on.

"Hey, mister, where you want me to put this stuff?" the truck driver asked Jax this time.

"Over there by the house." Jax pointed to where he wanted it to go.

"Whoa!" Caroline stopped the guy. "What's going on?"

"You need a new roof," Jax said, then pointed to the truck. "You're getting a new roof. Guys, help him out so we can get out of here," Jax shouted to Blaze and Hunter.

"Wait a minute!" Caroline shouted. Blaze and Hunter dropped the skids of shingles they were carrying and the truck driver turned off his small forklift. "I didn't order this."

"No, I did," Jax replied, shouting back at the men. "Come on, let's go."

"Stop!" Caroline shouted right back. The men grumbled and cursed, dropping the skid and even the truck driver got in a few curses. "How much was this stuff?"

"Not nine thousand, I can tell you that." Jax turned to yell at the guys again, but they waited, staring at Caroline.

She gave up. Jax was hardheaded and he wasn't going to leave here until what he ordered was off the truck. Hopping out of the way as Hunter and Blaze passed, Caroline couldn't do anything but watch.

"You going to the party tonight?" Blaze asked as he passed.

"Oh, I don't know." Caroline frowned, actually wanting to go, but knew she shouldn't. "I've got a lot to do here so probably not."

"Ah, come on." Hunter walked by, carrying more than the guy on the forklift. "This is kind of a going-away party for me."

"Going-away party?" Caroline followed Hunter where he put his load down. "Where you going?"

"Guess my little stunt of letting my wolf out on the City Hall steps wasn't such a great idea." Hunter snorted. "I've been ordered home to face the consequences." Hunter passed her.

"Do you have to go?" Caroline was a little sad that Hunter was leaving.

"When your Alpha calls, you go." Hunter stopped and walked backwards until he was next to Caroline. "Why, you going to miss me?"

"Hunter." Jax walked by and threw him a dirty look as he carried a stack of wood. "You may not make it back home if you don't get your ass in gear and help."

Hunter winked at her then took off. "Never fear, Caroline dear, I will be near if you ever have a need."

Jax turned quickly hitting Hunter in the head with a board. "Oh, my bad." Jax's evil grin clearly indicated he wasn't sorry at all.

Once everything was unloaded and Jax signed saying the material was delivered, the truck backed out.

"You guys go ahead." Jax wiped his hands on his jeans. "We'll be there in a few."

Once Blaze and Hunter were gone, Caroline looked behind her at all the material. "How much do I owe you?"

"I don't know." Jax shrugged. "You ready?"

"To hear how much I owe you? Yes, I am." Caroline stood, waiting.

"No," Jax said slowly. "To go to the party."

"No," Caroline said just as slow. "I have too much to do here."

"Everyone's expecting you. It would be rude for you not to show up." Jax tried not to grin in victory. "Very rude."

"Dammit!" Caroline almost stomped her foot, but didn't. Instead, she stomped her way into the house to change for the damn party. If she was anything, it wasn't rude and the ass was right; it would be very rude.

\*\*\*\*\*\*

Jax could tell Caroline was happy she had come. She was sitting and laughing with Pam and Nicole. He absolutely loved her laugh. Staying away from her would be safer for her, but he was a selfish son of a bitch and didn't want to stay away, couldn't stay away from her.

The women wanted to have a little get-together at the compound and it seemed like they all needed it.

"Well, it seems for once we got a win on our side." Jared walked up, tipping his beer in the air. "Finally."

Jax looked away from Caroline to Jill, who was glued to Slade's side. He couldn't blame Slade at all for keeping her near after almost losing her once. It had actually shaken him up seeing Jill lying helpless on the steps and the devastation on Slade's face. Something he definitely would never forget. He never thought love like that existed, but he had been proven wrong.

"If not for Jill, it wouldn't have happened," Jax replied

"Slade changing her on the steps of City Hall I think was the game changer. Now they are America's sweethearts. A true love story." Sid made a gagging sound. "Makes ya want to puke doesn't it."

Lana elbowed Sid in the stomach. "I think it was romantic and if I ever need to be changed I want it done on the City Hall steps."

"Honey, if I ever change you it will be in my bed with my…" Sid

185

started, but Lana covered his mouth with her hand blushing.

"Any word from your brother?" Jared asked Jax as Duncan joined them.

"No, but we will," Jax replied, taking a long drink of beer.

"What do you mean *we*?" Duncan asked, but everyone's attention turned to Jax.

"He's coming and we need to be ready." Jax looked at each one of them, then back to Caroline who looked up at him at that moment. "He doesn't play nice and will use whatever means necessary to take us down."

"What exactly happened between you and your brother?" Sid asked, eyeing Jax. "I mean we've dealt with a lot of mean bastards. What makes your brother any different?"

"He killed our sister." Jax straightened eyeing each Warrior surrounding him. "That's what makes him more dangerous than anyone we've ever dealt with. He doesn't give a fuck and he's coming. He's dangerously patient to the point you think he's moved on. He waits for the right time to strike and will take out anyone in his way."

With that said Jax left the group of Warriors to get another beer. His eyes caught Caroline who was watching his every move. He vowed right then and there his brother would never touch one hair on her head. Caroline Fitzpatrick was his and no one touched what was his.

# COMING SOON

'Lee County Wolves' Book #2

'The Protectors Series' Book #8 JAX

13578336R00109

Printed in Poland
by Amazon Fulfillment
Poland Sp. z o.o., Wrocław